MW00335412

Readers love
ANDREW GREY

Can't Live Without You

"This story was so fresh and new—and so well written and planned out, it was a pleasure to read from beginning to end."

—Alpha Book Club

"*Can't Live Without You* was like the best comfort food. It was feeling like your dreams were lost only to realize they were simply in hibernation."

—Diverse Reader

Eyes Only For Me
"

Andrew Grey manages to take an emotional rollercoaster of a love story and turn it into a teaching moment."

—Prism Book Alliance

"This is a good story, with well written, well developed characters. There are some seriously hot steamy scenes, and deeply profound dialogue between the main characters"

—*Divine Magazine*

Eyes Only For You

"Andrew Grey is truly a spectacular author and writes books that make an impact on the readers."

—Gay Book Reviews

More praise for
ANDREW GREY

Turning the Page

"The story telling is straightforward, the character of Malcolm relatable, and the ending—with a surprise twist and an element of danger—is quite satisfying."

—Gay.Guy.Reading and Friends

"The story was told very realistically. I felt for these characters."

—Two Chicks Obsessed

Chasing the Dream

"This is a wonderful story of a reverse rags-to-riches."

—The Blogger Girls

"I loved it from beginning to end!"

—Rainbow Book Reviews

Rekindled Flame

"Definitely a well done and uplifting story."

—My Fiction Nook

"*Rekindled Flame* is another well written story from Andrew Grey. There's danger and suspense and, as always, there's that great feeling of camaraderie, support and a sweet HEA."

—The Novel Approach

Published by DREAMSPINNER PRESS
www.dreamspinnerprss.com

Published by DREAMSPINNER PRESS
www.dreamspinnerpress.com

THE
PLAYMAKER
ANDREW GREY

Published by
DREAMSPINNER PRESS

5032 Capital Circle SW, Suite 2, PMB# 279, Tallahassee, FL 32305-7886 USA
www.dreamspinnerpress.com

This is a work of fiction. Names, characters, places, and incidents either are the product of author imagination or are used fictitiously, and any resemblance to actual persons, living or dead, business establishments, events, or locales is entirely coincidental.

The Playmaker
© 2016 Andrew Grey.

Cover Art
© 2016 L.C. Chase.
http://www.lcchase.com
Cover content is for illustrative purposes only and any person depicted on the cover is a model.

All rights reserved. This book is licensed to the original purchaser only. Duplication or distribution via any means is illegal and a violation of international copyright law, subject to criminal prosecution and upon conviction, fines, and/or imprisonment. Any eBook format cannot be legally loaned or given to others. No part of this book may be reproduced or transmitted in any form or by any means, electronic or mechanical, including photocopying, recording, or by any information storage and retrieval system, without the written permission of the Publisher, except where permitted by law. To request permission and all other inquiries, contact Dreamspinner Press, 5032 Capital Circle SW, Suite 2, PMB# 279, Tallahassee, FL 32305-7886, USA, or www.dreamspinnerpress.com.

ISBN: 978-1-63477-863-3
Digital ISBN: 978-1-63477-864-0
Library of Congress Control Number: 2016913022
Published November 2016
v. 1.0

Printed in the United States of America
∞
This paper meets the requirements of
ANSI/NISO Z39.48-1992 (Permanence of Paper).

To all my amazing fans,
and especially Pam Kay and Gloria Lakritz—I love you all!!!!

CHAPTER 1

"HUNTER DAVIS!" The voice rang like a bell through the house, followed by the front door slamming hard enough to rattle the pictures on the walls. "So help me God, if you aren't dressed, I'm going to come up there and drag you to this meeting naked if I have to." Heavy footsteps sounded on the stairs as Hunter stepped into his second shoe.

"Take a pill, Garvin. I'm almost ready." Hunter tied his shoe and then grabbed his jacket as his agent burst into the bedroom.

"Do you have any idea how pathetic this is?" Garvin strode to the edge of the bed. "If I set up a meeting, I have to pick your sorry ass up because I can't trust you to get there punctually. You never get your ass anywhere on time. I'm surprised that you get to practice or your games and that half that huge salary I negotiated for you isn't eaten up with late fines."

"I'm ready, see?" Hunter had heard all this before.

"We should have been on the road ten minutes ago," Garvin said flatly. "So get in the car. Traffic is terrible, and the Sure-Kill is already bad." Garvin turned and left the room. Hunter sighed and tamped down his frustration. "Do you want this endorsement deal or do I give it to Morris? At least he can get somewhere—anywhere—when he's supposed to." Garvin called out his name again, and Hunter hurried after him and down the stairs to the front door.

"It'll be fine. If I know you, the meeting is half an hour later than what you told me and we have plenty of time."

Garvin whipped around in a full fury. "That's your problem. You always think that everyone is playing you. I'm not your father or your mommy. I'm your agent, and I'm getting tired of being your fucking babysitter. Do you understand? I have clients who say they don't want to deal with you because they never know when you'll show. So pull your head out of your ass. On the football field, you may be a big man,

1

but this is real life, and believe it or not, these people's time is worth a hell of a lot more than yours, and they can replace you with a million other players who are all itching for deals like the ones I push your way." Garvin opened the door and stormed out of the house. Hunter followed, closing the door behind him, then strode to the car.

"Who pissed in your Cheerios?" Hunter pulled open the passenger door to the Lexus and slid into the comfortable seat.

"You did," Garvin chastised after slamming his door and starting the engine. "I have better things to do than drive all the way out here, pick you up, and then drive back into the city because you can't be bothered to get anywhere on time. It's pathetic on your part." He pulled out of the drive as fast as he dared, and they weaved through surface streets to the freeway into Philadelphia. Traffic was bumper-to-bumper, and Garvin drummed his fingers on the steering wheel. "What the hell am I going to do with you?" Garvin said, and Hunter realized he was really pissed at him this time. They'd had this conversation multiple times, but he always thought he and Garvin were friends of a sort. They went to basketball games together, and Hunter got him tickets whenever he needed them. Hell, he'd gotten Garvin's son in to meet all the players and showed him around.

"Come on...."

"I'm serious. I don't have time to be your chauffeur and timekeeper. I'm a busy man, and I have other clients besides you." The cars in front of them began to move, and Garvin loosened up a little. He pressed some buttons and talked to the car, instructing it to make a call.

"Helen, call over to Donnelly's office and tell his assistant that we're on our way. Traffic is a mess, but we'll be there as soon as we can." The cars picked up speed. "Hallelujah," Garvin said as he checked the time. "We should be on time, but you never know."

"Will do," Helen said. "And we got a call back from Johnston. He's interested." She was likely being vague on purpose because she knew Garvin was in the car with Hunter.

2

"Wonderful, set up the meeting for as soon as possible. I want to jump on this before someone else does." Garvin hung up, and Hunter turned to him, eyebrows raised expectantly. "That isn't for you."

"Why not?" Hunter asked. He knew that Johnston was a huge name in fashion and that Garvin had been working on a deal with them.

"Those people won't put up with your lateness. I was thinking of Thomlinson," Garvin said, speeding up the car. They were finally moving at near freeway speed, so Garvin relaxed. It seemed they weren't going to be late.

"Why?"

"Because he can be everywhere I schedule him, on time, and he's organized. If I were to offer you up as a model, they'd expect you to be wherever they needed you on time and even early. I don't think you've been early for anything in your life. That's a demanding business, and they require punctuality."

"But, Garvin, that's a sweet deal and you know it." Hunter was getting excited. He'd been the one to push Garvin to look into it. He couldn't take it away from him. "What do I have to do?"

Garvin took the first downtown exit and drove through exasperating city traffic before pulling into a parking garage. "You really want this? Because they've seen you in pictures and they are smitten. Your ass and package will be featured on billboards in Times Square a hundred feet tall if this works out."

"Yeah, I want to do this. It's every gay boy's dream." He remembered drooling over underwear models when he was too young to get porn.

"And we need to take advantage of you being gay to maximize promotional deals. You aren't the first gay player in professional football, but you are the first to hit it big and overcome the stigma. Everybody knows, and nobody really seems to care much." Garvin pulled up to the valet window, putting the car in park. Then he turned to Hunter, as serious as a heart attack. "If you want this deal, I'll do my best to get it, but I have a price. You will hire an assistant. You need to get organized and to keep yourself together."

3

"I don't want a stranger poking around in my business," Hunter said right away, drawing up his lip.

"What business? You can't find shit in that chaos of a room you call an office. If I hadn't arranged for a business manager to pay your bills, you'd have fucking lost your house by now. I'm tired of running your life for you. It's time you grew up, took responsibility, and saw to it that your life was more than you doing whatever you want to do at any given minute. And maybe having someone else will help. The day will come when you can't play, and then you won't be important any longer. You'll just be a former football player without any money coming in, unless you can land a job, and guess what, to do that you have to be able to show the fuck up on time." Garvin pounded the steering wheel once. "Am I finally getting through to you?"

Hunter had never seen Garvin like this. He was usually the most controlled and levelheaded man he knew. "Okay. Cool down. I'll get an assistant. But I want a woman who knows football." He didn't want a guy who would act strangely around him. The other players on the team had largely been understanding and hadn't given him too much grief for being gay, but some of the fans hadn't been too happy before he'd helped win some games. Still, he didn't want trouble brought into his house, and Hunter had always had good luck with the women in his life.

"Fine, but we're hiring an assistant, not a maid to clean up after you." Garvin opened his door and got out, handed the keys to the waiting valet, and got his case, while Hunter got out and waited for Garvin to join him.

"I know that."

"You need one of those too," Garvin said. "You know, for a gay guy, you're a complete slob."

"I am not." He kept the main portion of his house very clean. Yes, he'd be the first to admit that he wasn't organized and that his office was a mess, but the rest of his house wasn't. He had taken Garvin's advice and bought a nice house but not a huge mansion with more rooms than he'd ever need. "And stereotyping is not attractive."

Garvin pulled open the door to the office building, and Hunter walked inside. They were met by Mr. Donnelly's assistant, who escorted them up to one of the top floors and through to the conference room for their meeting.

"YOU WERE awesome," Garvin said when they were safe in the car again. "They loved you, and I honestly never thought they would want a gay spokesperson for their sporting-goods stores. Usually guys like them go with safe and secure, and you're anything but that."

"I'm also a damn good football player and a household name."

"With no ego whatsoever," Garvin quipped. "It was your personality that won them over. They could see you signing footballs in their stores and talking to people in a way they could relate to. That's what clinched the deal. Well, that and the fact that you aren't seen going into every gay bar and bathhouse in town. You may be gay and they know it, but you act like anyone else."

"I know. You said to keep my playing around quiet and out of town." There were plenty of guys interested in a night in the sack with him, but Hunter spent most of his nights alone. Hell, he spent all of his nights alone, if he was being honest. "But there hasn't been any."

Garvin pulled out of the garage and turned onto the city street. "Why?" he asked, clearly surprised. "Every player I know goes a little wild once they figure out that the money and fame bring more girls, in your case guys, than they can shake a stick at, and they go a little nuts at the buffet of flesh that's suddenly on display. Why haven't you?"

Hunter turned to look out the window. Not that he was seeing anything that passed by. "Because they aren't the guy I want." He knew it was past time to get over Michael and everything that had gone down his senior year in college, but... he hadn't really thought about it at all during the season. He'd been too damn busy learning the ropes and making sure he made a name for himself on the field. Now that the season was over and the preseason hadn't quite started yet, he had plenty of time, but…. "Things ended badly the last time, and I'm not ready for someone new."

"What about fucking? I know how it goes with players. You get really keyed up and the testosterone makes you higher than a kite. All you want to do is fuck like hell once the game is over."

Hunter wriggled his fingers and then wiped his hand on Garvin's coat just to see him squirm. That was funny as all hell. "I can control my own urges. I'm not some animal." The truth was, he wanted one and only one person, but he couldn't have him, and his heart wasn't going to allow him to move on, at least not the hell yet. It sucked like crazy, but those were the facts, and he wasn't able to change them.

"I didn't say that, and I'm thrilled that there hasn't been anything unseemly. That makes my job easier, and your publicists love you because they can spend their time building up your image rather than trying to do damage control. But I don't want you to be alone all the time either."

"It doesn't matter. I'm starting to think I'm one of those guys who's looking for something that just doesn't exist." He shrugged.

"Things must have been pretty bad if you haven't been with anyone since then," Garvin commented. "Now, mind you, no matter what, I don't want any details. I prefer to deal with girl parts, thank you, and I'm not interested in anything graphic, but if you want to talk, I'll do my best to listen."

"I can talk all I want, but there isn't anything that will change it," Hunter explained. "What's past is past, and it's best left there."

Garvin pressed buttons on his steering wheel and soon he was on the phone with Helen once again. "Go ahead and set up the Johnston meeting with myself and Hunter. Tell them he's interested. I'd like to move on this. Also call that agency and see if we can get some candidates out to Hunter's this week. He'd like a woman as his assistant, but at this point, we'll take what we can get."

"Is he there with you?" Helen asked.

"Yes, I'm here," Hunter said.

"Look, honey, I'll do my best, but it's discrimination for me to specifically request one gender over another. I'm sure there will be plenty of women who apply, but you cannot make that kind of request. Also, as a heads-up, you can't tell any of the male applicants that you wanted a woman. It could get you in trouble. Just play it cool and I think you can have what you want."

If Garvin had said that, Hunter would have fought him, but Helen was awesome, and there was no way he could argue with her. Besides, she was amazing, and always kind and thoughtful. And she always called him sweetheart or honey, which reminded him of home, and he liked that. "Okay. I'll be a good boy and play by the rules."

"Awesome. I'll get in touch with the agency as soon as I get off the phone."

"Unless you want the job," Hunter quipped. He'd steal her away from Garvin without a second thought if he thought he could.

"You know I'd take you up on your offer in a heartbeat, but then Garvin wouldn't know his butt from a hole in the ground, and where would you and all his other clients be? So I have to stay with him or otherwise the rest of your life would suffer, and I know you don't want that."

"Go back to work before I dock your pay," Garvin said with a smile and hung up. "She loves me."

"I'm sure she does. But what would your wife think if she found out?"

"Marie already thinks Helen and I are joined at the hip. Thank God Helen is too smart to get involved with me, and her Marine husband would cut my nuts off if anything improper was so much as thought about, let alone actually happened."

"You can say all you like, but you love Marie to death and would never do anything to hurt her." Hunter had seen the two of them together on more than one occasion and knew Garvin adored his wife—there was no doubt about it.

"Yes, I do," Garvin said with a sigh. "I need to get right back to the office, otherwise we could go to lunch, but when Helen calls with the assistants, try to be ready on time for their appointments. Also, unless you want them to run screaming from the house, try to clean up that pigsty you call an office."

"Why?" Hunter asked.

"Because they'll need somewhere to work and the office is the most logical place. What did you want to do, have a phone installed in one of the bathrooms so they can work and take a shit at the same time?"

"They'll be at my house?" Hunter hadn't thought of that.

"Of course. She'll be your assistant. That means she'll be seeing to your schedule and running other errands, like making sure your cleaning gets picked up. Maybe, if you're lucky, you'll be able to find someone who can help you pick out an outfit that isn't a pair of tan pants and a blue shirt. I think I've already seen this outfit, like, every time I see you."

"What's wrong with my clothes? You said I should dress nice for the meeting. I didn't think you meant a suit and tie."

"I didn't. But you only have one of those, and it's a dark suit that you wear with a blue shirt and a red tie. I swear you only have barely more than one color in your closet. Do you get the picture? It wouldn't hurt to spiff up your image a little, and maybe your assistant can help with that."

"Fine. I'll clean out the office and go through all the stuff in there. Have Helen schedule the potential assistants for no earlier than tomorrow, and I'll be nice and find the best one."

Garvin coasted into Hunter's driveway and wound down his window after Hunter got out. "I'll be in touch with the time for the Johnston meeting. I expect it to be a few days, and this time, please don't make me come out here to get you. Just be sure to be there on time." Hunter turned away. "You know, if you wrote these things down, you wouldn't forget or be late." Garvin raised the window and backed out of the drive.

Hunter went into the house, dropped his keys on the side table, and pulled open the office door. He immediately closed it. Garvin was right. Hunter had used the room as a paperwork dumping ground for months. He went out to the garage and got a box for sorting.

THE FOLLOWING afternoon Hunter led his third interview to the door. "Thank you, Monica."

"I'm sure I'll love working for you," she said and stepped outside. Hunter made sure she got into her car, and then he closed the door and leaned against it.

Good Lord. All three of them had been the same. None had been serious possibilities—they had all seen "football player" and turned up looking more like cheerleaders than actual job applicants. Jocelyn, the first potential assistant, had been the most forceful and had actually insinuated that if they worked together well enough, maybe he'd give her a chance to rock his world and show him what he'd been missing. The second, Cindy, had been an improvement and even said she could cook, which he thought was nice. When he asked her what she made, Cindy told him she had the best vegan recipes and it was the only way to go. Of course she never soiled her hands with meat of any kind, didn't eat it, didn't want to be around or see it. Hunter figured buying his groceries would be impossible for her. Monica had been nice enough, but he couldn't see her as his assistant either. She had gone on and on about how she thought football was barbaric. She, of course, accepted that he was probably one of the good players and said she'd pray for him.

His phone rang and he saw it was Helen. "I just saw the last of the three out, and none of them was a fit. I'm not vegan, I play football, so I'm barbaric, and I don't want to be converted."

"Oh dear. I'll go down to the agency and see if they have anyone else who might be suitable. Sometimes things like this can take time. You don't think I found Garvin on my first try, do you? I interviewed a lot of bosses before I found one I didn't want to kill."

"You're hilarious," Hunter said, and she laughed and hung up. Hunter went into the living room and put in a CD of game footage his coach had sent over. There was no time like the present to learn about the new players he'd be up against come the start of the season.

CHAPTER 2

MONTGOMERY WILLIS strode into the employment agency with all the confidence he didn't have. He needed a job, or the tenuous life he'd been trying to hold on to would be gone and he'd have to start over. Or move home to live with his mother, which was about as interesting as oral surgery without Novocain.

"What skills do you have?" the woman behind the desk asked him once he'd finally been able to see an actual person.

"I'm organized, and I have computer skills. I worked as the receptionist in a law firm for six months." He did his best to smile. "I thought I was doing a good job for them."

"Why did you leave?" the woman asked. She was in her late thirties and dressed professionally. Monty thought she was nice-enough-looking.

"They said I didn't portray the image they wanted." Of course, that was their way of saying they didn't want a gay man out in the front and center of their big, prestigious law firm. He wrung his hands and waited for the next inevitable question.

"What about the job before that?"

"You mean working in the mail room. That didn't work out very well." *The guy in charge thought I was God's gift and couldn't keep his hands to himself? I'm sorry, but it isn't only ladies who have the problem with men with grabby hands. He said no one would believe me because he had a wife and kids at home and that if I didn't....* Monty swallowed and pulled his thoughts back where they belonged. He smiled as best he could. "Basically I've had the worst luck with jobs, but I need one really badly, and I work hard." He swallowed again and straightened his ascot. He figured there was no use pretending he was anything other than gay. He'd tried hiding it, but it always leaked

11

out around the edges, so to speak. He wasn't going to pretend to be something he wasn't.

"I see." She tapped the keys on her computer. "I don't really have anything at the moment." Her phone rang, and she groaned, signaling quiet with her finger before picking it up.

"Marlene," a man said on the other side of the line. He spoke a little loudly, and Monty had excellent hearing. "Do you have any other potential applicants as personal assistants for Mr. Davis?"

"I sent three out."

"They were interviewed, and the reports weren't good." He sounded exasperated. "Helen Grosvenor is here now to see if there is anyone else available."

"I'd make a great personal assistant," Monty said, speaking up. He'd take anything at this point, and whoever this Mr. Davis was, being his assistant couldn't be all that hard.

Marlene looked at Monty, then said into the phone, "I have a potential candidate. Helen can talk to him and judge for herself." She hung up, and a few minutes later, a nervous man appeared in the doorway.

"Please follow me," the man said to Monty. "Do you have copies of your résumé?"

Monty grabbed his well-worn leather case and pulled out a copy. The man took it without looking at it and led the way through to a small conference room off to the side. "Please have a seat." He left the room, and Monty sat down, wondering what he was getting himself into.

A few minutes later, a stunning woman in a blue dress, who had beautiful eyes and perfectly done hair, came in and sat down.

"Hello, Mr. Willis, my name is Helen Grosvenor. Have you had any experience as a personal assistant?" she asked after she'd shaken his hand.

"No, I haven't. But I have worked in an office where I had to get the coffee and run the errands of a half-dozen people when their assistants couldn't come into work. I'm organized, and I have my own car, such as it is. I can take care of whatever Mr. Davis wants."

He kept his hands in his lap and did his best not to rub them together. His nervous energy rose by the second, and his right leg bounced under the table.

She looked over the résumé and then up at him, her eyes widening a little. "Mr. Davis is looking for someone with discretion. Have you ever handled sensitive information?"

"I worked in a law office, and there were times when conversations were overheard. I treated each and every one as though the information was confidential and never talked about it with anyone, and I still won't now." He lifted his chin.

"How are you with fashion?"

Monty stood so she could see what he was wearing. He knew he looked good in his gray slacks and lime-green shirt. "I have my own personal style, but I have helped many people with their shopping." He knew he looked good and smiled when she nodded appreciatively. "I don't believe everyone should look the same. Each person must find a style they're comfortable with." He turned to her. "Your work attire is impeccable, and you wear that shade of blue beautifully. But I'm willing to bet when you let your hair down—and my guess is that it flows to your shoulders—and put on a dress—say, in red—you turn every head in the room." He didn't grin when she smiled. He knew he'd been right. "But that eye shadow is wrong for you. I know you were trying to coordinate with the dress, but you have amazing brown eyes and you should be bringing them out instead." He hoped he hadn't gone too far.

"You really think so?"

"Yes. You have stunning eyes, so don't hide them."

She cleared her throat and returned her attention to his résumé. "Look, Mr. Davis is… someone important…. I think you'll do nicely. I'll set up an interview with him at his home for tomorrow, is that all right?" Monty nodded. "He's going to need some convincing, but I think you'll be perfect." She smiled and stood up. "Here's my card, and here's the address. You need to be there at ten tomorrow morning. And please be on time."

"I take it Mr. Davis is a stickler."

13

Mrs. Grosvenor shook her head. "Mr. Davis can't seem to get anywhere on time. That's part of why he needs you. So be punctual to set an example. Good luck. I'm afraid you're going to need it."

Monty stood, thanked her for the chance, and left the conference room with Mrs. Grosvenor behind him. He nearly ran into Marlene along the way. He filled her in on what was happening, and she brought him back to her desk so he could fill out some paperwork for her. Then he left the office, still clutching the cards Mrs. Grosvenor had given him, as though they were a lifeline.

He left the employment office feeling a little better than he had when he'd come in. At least he'd gotten an interview out of it. That was something.

He walked to the corner and descended the stairs to the nearest subway station, scanned his pass, and weaved through the various tunnels until he got to the proper platform and then took his train home.

Monty hadn't lied about owning a car. He just hadn't told the whole truth. His car, Lizzie, was a piece of crap that sometimes started and sometimes decided, like it had that morning, to sit there and do jack shit.

Of course once he arrived at the apartment he shared with two other people and checked out the car, the damn thing started with no problem at all. He wanted to swear and curse at Lizzie, but he knew he had to treat her with respect or the old bitch would leave him stranded by the side of the road when he needed her the most.

He turned off the car and locked her up. "Please cooperate tomorrow and get me where I want to go." He wasn't above pleading. Then he went inside. As he shut the door, a shuffle from behind caught his attention, and he spun around.

"How did it go?" his sister, Emily, asked from the sofa. He wasn't expecting her to be home from summer school already. It must have been a teacher in-service day or something.

"I got an interview for a personal-assistant job." He hung his jacket in the closet and joined her. "It's only an interview, but the person I talked to said I was perfect for it."

14

"Then why aren't you jumping off the walls?"

"Because I don't have the job yet. And hopefully he's not a perv. I've been perved on plenty, and let me tell you, if I got this job, it would be great not to have to worry about Mr. Wandering Hands or sucking some guy's dick to stay employed." Monty shuddered. "And he was old, like almost sixty… and ugly… let's not forget ugly."

"Not that you'd do something like that anyway. You have too good a heart, and you'd never be able to live with yourself. Now me on the other hand, I'd make him think I was going to do that, and then, when I had his nuts in my hand, I'd yank the things down to his ankles until they swung like a fucking pendulum." The feral gleam in her eyes made him smile.

"You would too." He leaned back and put his feet up on the old, beat-up coffee table. "Where's your other half?"

"Camille's out getting some milk and stuff." Emily sighed. Those two were so much in love, it fucking hurt. Monty wanted what they had so badly he could taste it. They'd been together for two years now and were talking about getting married and then having kids. They had even asked if he'd act as the father, so to speak. She and Camille had figured, with Camille carrying the child and him as the father, that was as close as possible to them to have a baby biologically, and he'd do anything for his sister. "So what time is your interview?"

"Ten, and I need to go out to the Main Line. I was thinking of taking the train, but it would be so much easier if Lizzie would cooperate. I was told to be on time, so I'll leave extra early just in case."

"You really want this?"

"How in the hell should I know, Em? I need to work, and every job I get looks good at first and then turns to complete shit before my eyes. I need to support myself and not live off my big sister any longer. You know I love you, but you and Camille need to have a place for yourselves, especially if the two of you have a child."

"You know you're welcome here as long as you need."

"Maybe, but I won't sponge off the two of you, and I need to pay my way." His pride was at stake. "The thought of going back to Mother is enough to make me do just about anything to make it work."

"God, I can imagine. All that cooking and cleaning, all those chores while Mom reads or watches television and doesn't lift a finger whenever she's home from work…? Yeah, the thought of going back to that would be more than I could stand."

"See. So I'll take this interview and do my best to win over this Mr. Davis. He's supposed to be some kind of celebrity, but God knows what that means in this town. Maybe he's one of those guys who does the news or something." Monty got up and went to his room. He changed into jeans and a loose T-shirt before going to the kitchen to start dinner. "How does pasta sound?"

"Carbonara?" Em asked from the living room.

"I can do that." Monty got out the ingredients and began chopping and preparing them for the sauce.

Camille came home as he was working. He heard the two of them in the other room, giggling and snogging loudly. Monty let them have their time together as he worked. It wasn't like he wanted to see his sister and her girlfriend going at it. He was happy they were happy, and that was enough of an exploration of their mating habits.

"Em says you're cooking." Camille bounced into the kitchen a few minutes later. Monty put the pasta on to boil and picked up a spoon to stir the sauce.

"Yup. She asked for your favorite."

"You're good to us." Camille hugged him, and he set his utensils aside to return it. She made his sister happy and that was enough for Monty to like her, but Camille was also an extraordinary person who he liked on her own merits. She was an amazing woman with a huge heart and a backbone of steel and stunning to look at with ebony skin, silky black hair, and eyes as black as coal but always filled with warmth.

"I try." He turned back to the stove. "How was work?"

Camille groaned. "Sometimes I wonder why I went into this line of work." She poured two glasses of white wine and one of water. She asked if he wanted some, then handed him one of the glasses and took the water for herself. "I thought social work would be helping people, but it's all bullshit paperwork to navigate a labyrinth of bureaucracy designed not to help anyone but make it look like they are." She sipped from her glass and went to take the other wineglass in to Em. "I hear you have an interview."

"Yup. Keep those long, beautiful fingers and nails of yours crossed for me. It's going to be an uphill battle." He picked a knife from the holder and returned to making dinner.

At eight thirty the following morning, he got into his car and crossed his fingers and said nice things to Lizzie, and she started as though nothing had ever been wrong.

"Thank you, girl." He pulled out of his parking spot and made his way toward the address he'd been given.

It took him nearly half an hour of nail-biting driving before he was near where he was supposed to be, which meant he was an hour early. So he stopped at a coffee shop and used the time to read one of their newspapers and to enjoy a skinny latte. Then, at about twenty till, he drove the rest of the way, arriving a little early, but he'd been told to be on time, so early was good, right? He parked and walked to the front door, rang the bell and waited.

The door opened, and Monty nearly dropped his coffee and briefcase. In front of him was an example of manhood who could only be described as a god, and this god wore nothing but a towel, showing off broad shoulders, a narrow waist, and natural blond hair, judging by the treasure trail that disappeared behind the towel that Monty wished would just fall away. Oh God, he was in so much trouble if this was the guy he was supposed to interview with.

"Yeah," the man barked.

"I'm Monty Willis. Are you Mr. Davis? I was told to be here at ten for an interview." He tried not to look at him, but it was hard knowing where to look with all that on display. He swallowed hard and figured the guy's face was a safe place. He was wrong. High cheekbones, a jaw cut from granite, and cobalt blue eyes. In other words, this was a dream man standing right in front of him, complete with pecs for days and a stomach that Monty would never have, even if he did a million crunches every day for the rest of his life.

"You're early." The man stepped back and turned around. "Have a seat in the living room. I'll get changed and be back down. Please don't spill your coffee."

Monty stepped forward. "I got this one for you. I wasn't sure how you liked it so I got black, but I have some sugar and one of those little creamer things if you need one." He handed the cup over.

"Thank you. Black is fine," he said less forcefully and climbed the stairs. It took all Monty's willpower not to whistle at the way the towel clung to a butt that he was sure was hard enough to crack walnuts.

Monty sat in a masculine-looking living room with dark leather furniture and white walls. "Jesus, I've either died and gone to gay heaven, or this is payback for all the times I've undressed subway guys in my mind." He fanned himself to get under control and then remembered why he was here. He pulled out his résumé, the one he'd reworked last night so it sounded more appropriate for a personal assistant, and set it on the table. Then he waited for Mr. Davis to return, hoping he had enough time to recover from the sight so he didn't babble.

"As I said, you showed up early." Mr. Davis came into the room.

"Only ten minutes, and to be early is to be on time, to be on time is to be late, and to be late is unforgivable because it shows disrespect for others." Monty immediately wondered why the hell his mouth never stayed shut when it should.

"Okay, then. Hunter Davis." He extended his hand, and Monty jumped to his feet.

"Monty Willis. My real name is Montgomery, but I hate it, so everyone calls me Monty." He shook his hand and sat back down. "I talked to Mrs. Grosvenor from your agent's yesterday, and she said you were looking for an assistant, and she thought I might do for what you needed."

"Helen said that?" Hunter sat down as well and picked up Monty's résumé. "Okay." He dropped the page back onto the table and stared at him. "Do you know who I am?"

Monty shook his head. "Should I?" God, he was blowing it badly.

"Ever watch football?"

"No. I mean I have, but only on occasion." And only for the shots where they showed the guys in those tight uniforms that showed off their bubble butts, but he kept that to himself. "Is that important?"

"I'm a receiver for the Philadelphia Red Hawks." He lifted his gaze, and Monty was sure he was about to get kicked out of here at any second.

"Sorry. But is knowing that a requirement for being your assistant? What else do you need? I'm very organized, and Mrs. Grosvenor said you needed someone to manage your schedule for you. I can do that. I have a car, so I can run errands and get stuff for you. She also said you were interested in some help picking out some new looks."

"I look just fine," Hunter said testily, and Monty was seconds from just excusing himself and getting ready to go. Mrs. Grosvenor had been right—this was an uphill battle, and he was completely blowing it. Since he had little to lose, he decided to go for it.

"Is that what you usually wear?" Monty asked.

"Yeah." Hunter glared at him. "Why?"

"It's a little dated and guy frumpy. You're a football player, right? You should look good when you go out. I mean, this says middle-aged dad in the park, or even grandpa with the grandkids. You would look amazing in a nice pale green with some cool jeans, or maybe a pair of dress slacks and a silk shirt. And your hair." Monty *tsk*ed. "I bet you go to a place like Supercuts or something. You have great hair that, with a proper cut, could look amazing." He wanted to touch it to see if his hair was as soft as it looked.

"So you'd change me," Hunter said.

"No. I'm saying I'd work with you to bring out your style."

"Okay." Hunter clearly wasn't buying it. "Do you cook?"

"Yeah."

"What kind of food?" Hunter demanded.

"What do you like? I made fettuccine carbonara last night for dinner, I make killer pork chops, and I've been told my chicken wings are to die for. But I bake them so they don't have all the fat. I make a mean cheesecake and cupcakes too."

"What about vegan?"

"Are you vegan?" He somehow doubted it, as big as Hunter was.

"God, no."

"Then why ask? I'll cook all the meat your football heart desires if you'll give me a chance." He thought he might have earned a few points.

"What about cleaning?"

"I'm not a maid. I'm your assistant. If you want me to find you a cleaning service, I can certainly do that."

"Okay. That's great, but you don't know football. Do you have any idea when preseason starts?" Monty shook his head. "Practice schedules? Do you have any idea about the demands on my time once practice starts? How about conditioning. Do you run?"

"Yeah. That I can do. Where do you need me to go for you?" Monty realized he'd misunderstood as soon as he saw the sneer.

"I mean run as in exercise."

"Oh. I used to run in school," Monty answered. "Look, I may not be the kind of person you're looking for, but I'll do my very best for you if you'll give me a chance." He was still trying to figure out what Hunter was looking for.

Hunter sighed. "Fine, I'll give you a chance. I need you to put together my schedule for me. You can call Helen to get the things from my agent. You'll also need to contact my publicist as well as the coach's office and the team office. I also have a bunch of laundry upstairs that will need to be taken care of, and I have a team meeting sometime this week. Oh, and I have a lunch this afternoon, but I can't remember what time or with who. It's just some vague memory. So find out for me. I need a cleaning service, so get on that, and I'll need someone to open the pool and clean the hot tub. It's smelling funky."

Monty had grabbed a notebook in his bag and scribbled things down as Hunter had rattled them off.

"Also, when you talk to Helen, tell her that I hired you on probation for a month, and we'll see how we go from there. You can work in the office over there, and you'll need to go through everything in it to make sure there's nothing important that I missed." Hunter stood and left the room, but returned a few seconds later like he'd forgotten something. Monty was just catching up on his notes. "One more thing. You are never to talk about anything in my life with anyone else. If the press show up, no comment. If someone asks you about me at the grocery store, no comment. If you're in a restaurant and a game is on, you don't tell anyone you work for me. You got that? No one."

"Okay, but why?"

"Because people want to know what's going on in my private life. And it's none of their business. I may be one of the first gay players in the league, and everyone thinks that gives them the right to know everything about me. Just so we're clear. You open your mouth, and you're out the door on your tight little ass." Hunter left the room and went up the stairs.

Monty made sure he had all his notes and then called Helen. "This is Monty, we talked at the employment agency yesterday," he said once she answered. "Hunter said to call and tell you that I got the job on probation."

"Good. Are you at Hunter's?"

"Yes. And he says he has a lunch meeting today with someone he can't remember at a time he can't remember."

Helen huffed. "That sounds like him. I'll find out what that is, and I'll call you back. In the meantime I'm sending a messenger over with a laptop and a phone for you to use, and I'll add you to his personal e-mail account, which he rarely checks. I can forward a list of contacts for him as well."

"Oh thank God." He'd been wondering where he was supposed to dig up the numbers of all the people Hunter had rattled off.

"Don't worry about it. If you can get that man where he's supposed to be most of the time, Garvin and I will fly you to Hawaii for your vacation. I'll also set up an e-mail account specifically for you, and I'll send all the information there. I'll have it delivered with the equipment. Just relax, and don't let him get to you."

"Thanks." He got up and paced a little nervously.

"No problem, just watch for the delivery, and I'll text you at this number when I figure out about his lunch." She hung up, and Monty went to find the office.

The desk was empty and clean, as were the other surfaces.

"Clearing this task should be easy," he said, looking at his list and his note about taking care of the office contents. Then Monty walked around behind the desk and stumbled over three boxes laid out on the floor. He opened the first one and groaned. The box was filled with what looked like random receipts, statements, and pieces of paper. This was going to take some time, like a month of Sundays.

CHAPTER 3

HUNTER WAS dressed and ready, standing in the front hall.

"Monty," he called, and the door to his office opened. "Did you figure out this whole lunch thing?"

"It isn't lunch. You're supposed to meet with a photographer at two for a calendar shoot. Here's the address." He handed Hunter a Post-it note, and Hunter stared at it. "Do you want me to program it into your GPS?"

"Yeah, do that." Hunter handed it back. "I'm taking the BMW in the garage. Here are the keys." He tossed them at Monty, who dropped them on the floor. Heaven help him, he'd gotten an assistant who couldn't catch. What the hell other stuff wasn't he able to do? "I'm also going out to dinner with some of the other players. So I'll be leaving at six. Can you make something for me to bring? It's poker night."

"I can do that. What time are you supposed to be there?" Monty asked.

"I said six," Hunter reiterated, and Monty blinked at him. "What?" He was getting testy.

"You said you had to leave at six. Where is the party?"

"In Paoli somewhere. I know the way." Hunter was getting exhausted with this. "Just make something, please."

"Okay. So if you're supposed to be there at six, I'll have something ready for you at five thirty. Do you want me to call and remind you?" Monty grabbed Hunter's phone from his hand, put in a number, and called himself. "There. Now we each have the numbers we need." He turned and went toward the garage.

Hunter watched him go, that tiny rear end slowly moving back and forth. See, this was the reason he'd asked for a woman. Monty was obviously gay and as cute as they came. This whole thing was

23

going to drive Hunter crazy. The last thing he wanted was someone in his business, questioning everything he did. But even more, he wanted someone who didn't have eyes like warm chocolate and a smile as bright as the warm sun.

He sat at one of the barstools at the kitchen island and made a call. "Garvin, I really hate this. This assistant, Monty, has been here three hours and he's already getting in my way. I tell him something, and he asks me a bunch of shit and then tells me something different." He knew he was whining, but he had to get Garvin behind him.

"What did he do?"

"He was asking about when I had to be somewhere. I know what time I have to leave."

"Your assistant was asking you what time you had to be somewhere and where it was?"

"Yeah. Then he told me when I had to leave."

"Well, praise the Lord. I'm going to church tonight to light a candle. Jesus, Hunter, he's trying to make sure you get places on time. That's his job. You've nearly killed deals because you were late. That's why you hired him. I was serious the day before yesterday— you either get your act together and pull your head out of your ass, or so help me, I'll hand you over to one of my staff and wash my hands of you. And if that happens, you can kiss things like the Johnston deal good-bye forever. You aren't the end-all, be-all you think you are. So quit your whining and let him help you."

Garvin hung up, and Hunter put his phone on the counter, seething. He schooled his expression when Monty came back inside.

"The address for your photo shoot is programmed into the car." Monty opened the refrigerator door and pulled out a plate. "I didn't have much time, and there wasn't much in the house, but I made you a sandwich and some chips for lunch. I hope that's okay."

"Thanks," Hunter said blankly as Monty left the room, clearly avoiding him, and returned to the office. Hunter ate in a hurry and checked his phone for the time. He ended up playing a game until he had to go.

"You need to go now," Monty said from the doorway. "And when you get the chance, we should go over some of this paperwork in the office. A lot of it appears to be garbage and junk mail that I shredded, but there is other stuff I wanted to check with you about before I destroy it."

"Okay. Put the things to go through aside."

"Is there anything else you need before you go?" The doorbell rang, and Monty hurried to the front door. "Oh thank goodness," Monty practically squealed, and Hunter wondered what was going on. He followed and saw Monty cradling two boxes in his arms. "You're a lifesaver." Monty closed the door and practically ran into him.

"What's all this? And why are you receiving deliveries here?" he demanded, his hands on his hips.

Monty looked like he'd been slapped. "It's some things Helen sent over for me." He stepped back and seemed to shrink. "She said I'd need a laptop and a phone." He set the boxes down, opened them, and pulled out a brand-new iPhone out of one and an iBook computer from the other, both still in their packaging.

"Oh." Hunter stalked away, feeling like an ass, but he wasn't going to let Monty see that. He grabbed his jacket and felt Monty looking him over. "What?" He glanced down at himself.

"Can we see if you have a shirt at least that doesn't look like something worn by Richie Cunningham?" Hunter wasn't sure what was so terrible about a plaid button-up and khakis.

"I have to go." He slipped on his jacket.

"You have five minutes. I was pushing you to be early."

Hunter huffed—he'd been doing that a lot lately—climbed the stairs, and took off his jacket as he stalked down the hallway. He went to his room with Monty right behind him and opened the closet.

Monty peered inside and turned back to him, looking aghast. "My God." He moved hangers aside and continued until he reached the very end of the closet. "Thank God. There is something decent in here." Monty pulled out a shirt that Hunter couldn't remember having, and handed it to him. "Put this on. I bet it will look nice on you. There isn't anything I can do with the pants, but at least...."

Hunter unbuttoned his shirt, and Monty went silent. Hunter took the new one off the hanger and shrugged it on. When he turned back to Monty, he glanced away quickly. "How does it feel?"

"Soft." Hunter buttoned it up and then started to tuck it in.

"No. Leave it out. It will look better, and the silk is way more appealing than those pants." Monty smoothed out the shirt and rolled up the cuffs, then stepped back and smiled. "Now you look like a million bucks." Monty tossed him the jacket. "Go get 'em."

"You're coming with me," Hunter said, and Monty squeaked and hurried out of the room and down the stairs. When Hunter caught up with him, he was pulling the phone out of its case and shoving it into his bag.

"You should have told me." Monty grabbed the computer as well, tucking it under his arm.

"I just decided that I might need something while I'm there."

Hunter went out to the car, and Monty followed and got into the passenger seat. He buckled up and then placed the computer on his lap and started working with it and his phone while Hunter drove.

"How can you do that and ride at the same time?"

"If you want me to be able to get your schedule together, and a lot of it is in here already, I need to get started and use all the time I have." He went back to working, and Hunter followed the GPS instructions to a studio on the outskirts of downtown. He parked, and Monty gathered his things and followed him inside.

"I'm going to need coffee," Hunter said, and Monty hurried off with his bag while Hunter climbed the stairs to an open loft-type space.

"Hunter, you look great, and we're really excited about what you're doing to help us," the charity-calendar director said. He'd met her briefly through his agent. "This is our photographer, Raphael." Hunter nodded and shook his hand.

The photographer cleared his throat. "Let's get started, shall we? You can undress behind the curtain. There's a robe you can put on while we finish setting up the shot."

"What do you want me to wear?" Hunter asked.

"Why, nothing but a smile and a towel draped just so. I thought you understood. This is a nude calendar. We aren't going to show anything important. It's meant to tantalize. Could you just get ready?"

Hunter didn't like this, and he pulled out his phone and called Garvin.

"Hunter…." He sounded pleased.

"I'm at the shoot, and they want me naked."

"Yeah. I sent you examples of last year's calendar when I asked if you'd do it. Let me guess—you didn't look at them."

Hunter ground his teeth. "It's fine." He hung up as Monty rushed up and placed a cup of coffee in his hand.

"What?"

"I need to get undressed." Hunter handed back the coffee, and Monty stepped back, shaking his head as Hunter went behind the screen, stripped off his clothes, and put on the robe. Then he stepped out and over to the photographer. "What would you like me to do?"

The photographer shifted his gaze.

Hunter followed it and stepped back on the set. "No way in hell. I am not standing in a bathtub." He stepped closer to the photographer. "I'm doing this for charity, but I'm not doing a bathtub because I don't bathe with a football, and I will have one, do you understand?"

He heard Monty snicker and sneered at him.

"That's…," Raphael began.

"Change it."

"How about using that statue in the corner?" Monty asked, and the photographer whirled around. *If looks could kill….*

"I'm the photographer."

Monty took a step back, and Hunter looked at the statue he'd mentioned. "Why not? I am not going to do this bathtub thing, so you can forget that altogether."

"Very well. Why do you think we should use the statue?" Raphael quipped, clearly humoring them, and Hunter was ready to smack him and walk the hell out of here.

27

"Look at it. Hunter has the same athletic build. He could stand half beside, half behind it, and the base would hide his bits. It would show his butt, and the sculpture would mirror him. He's an athlete, and so is that." Monty stepped back and made his way to a corner, seemingly trying to disappear while Raphael seemed to consider what he was saying. Monty relaxed as Raphael's expression softened.

"Give it a try." Raphael nodded, and his people began moving things around. Hunter got his coffee while he waited, and Monty did his best to try to hide out of the way. Once they were ready, Hunter set his coffee on a nearby table, took his place by the white marble statue, and Raphael got behind the camera. Everyone else left the studio area, and Hunter dropped his robe.

"This is really working," Raphael said as he moved around him, giving instructions and taking pictures. "You look great." He snapped image after image. "Just a few more. That's it, right there." He stopped and put the camera down. Hunter put the robe back on, and Raphael moved to the computer on the desk next to him. The images taken were displayed on the screen, and Raphael moved through them quickly until they found an image that leapt off the screen. "That's it. Right there."

The assistants came back in, and Monty put Hunter's coffee in his hand.

"That's hot," Monty said when he saw the image on the screen. "Go on and change." Hunter went back behind the screen. "Okay, I want to see every image," Monty demanded. "Delete that and that. You will not keep those images in any way. Delete them now!"

"That's not in the agreement," Raphael said.

"You'll do it, or so help me, I'll destroy the camera and throw the computer out the fucking window. Now get to it." Once Hunter had dressed, he came out from behind the screen to find Monty with his hands on his hips, glaring at Raphael. "That one too... and that one. Jesus, you're just a pervert, aren't you? Get rid of all of those, now." Raphael was seething, but he did as Monty wanted, and then Monty looked through the pictures that were left and did the same on the camera. "There better not be any backups to any of these."

"This is all of them," Raphael said, and Monty stepped back.

"Good. We want copies of all of these. They won't be published anywhere, but Hunter deserves copies of all of them."

"They'll be sent over once the calendar images are finalized," Raphael told Hunter, ignoring Monty. He handed Hunter a card, and he passed it to Monty.

"Thank you," Hunter said, and he waited while Monty gathered his things, and then they left the studio. "What was all the yelling about?" Hunter asked once they were on the stairs, heading for street level.

"He'd taken a bunch of pictures of you that included things that were best left unseen by the general public. I don't know if he'd delete them himself, but they didn't need to exist." Monty pulled open his door once Hunter unlocked the car. "Who knows where those pictures could end up in a few years? Look on the Internet—there are pictures of stars' privates all over the place. I didn't think you needed to join that club." Monty opened his computer and began tapping away as Hunter stared at him for a few seconds. He was trying to remember the last time someone other than Garvin had really looked out for him. He was about to say thank you when Monty looked up from what he was doing. "Are we going back to the house?"

"Yes. Why?"

"I need to make something for you to bring to your party and there is nothing in your house. I was going to go to the store while you were gone, but…." Monty sighed. "I can make something quickly."

"We can stop on the way home."

"Okay. Who are you playing poker with?"

"Mark, Clyde, Randall, and Joe." Hunter looked for some sort of recognition, but Monty simply blinked back at him. Hunter turned his attention back to the road. "They're on the team with me."

"Oh," Monty said and turned back to the computer. Hunter rolled his eyes and once again wondered how this was actually going to work.

He pulled into the nearest grocery store, drummed his fingers on the steering wheel, and watched the clock as Monty raced inside.

He told himself he wasn't going to watch him go, but damned if his gaze didn't follow him until he disappeared inside. True to his word, Monty was back out in ten minutes, carrying a bag in each hand. He set the groceries on the backseat and got back into the car. Monty buckled up as Hunter turned the key, and then they continued the drive home.

HUNTER HAD settled on the sofa to watch game films, but it wasn't really working. The scent of sweetness and chocolate drew him out of his seat and into the kitchen, like a siren song.

"I didn't have time to make my chocolate-cheesecake brownies, so I baked you some cookies to take instead. They're peanut butter chocolate chip." Hunter inhaled, and damn, his mouth watered. "I'm just taking them out. They'll need to cool, and then I can pack them up for you." Monty checked his watch. "I'm going to work on your schedule some more. I'll print out what you need for tomorrow." He set out sandwiches and Hunter tucked in.

Monty put the dishes away after they'd eaten and then went into the office without a word while Hunter leaned against the counter, watching his butt sway back and forth. He was so screwed.

Hunter needed to get a different assistant. That was all there was to it. Romantic entanglements, or at least lustful ones, were not in the cards. Fans knew he was gay, but they didn't want to know about it. He could play football, and as long as he kept his reputation clean, he was fine. But Hunter knew that having affairs or flaunting a parade of guys was not going to fly. And neither were rumors about him and his assistant. All Hunter had to do was look at Monty strangely in public and they would start.

Hunter closed his eyes and did his best to push away all the voices and differing opinions that swirled around, yelling over each other. He needed silence and concentration, but he only got that when he was playing, and training camp was still a month away.

"You need to leave in half an hour," Monty said from the other room, and Hunter groaned. He wasn't a child, and yet... damn, how could he argue with Monty when he'd already gotten lost in other thoughts and hadn't been paying attention to the time? Hunter *did* need a keeper after all.

The office door closed, and Hunter heard Monty climbing the stairs, most likely on his way to sort clothes.

He went back to watching the videos in the living room but gave up after only a few minutes. He sighed, grabbed a beer from the refrigerator, and headed upstairs.

"When was the last time you did laundry?" Monty asked as Hunter approached the open bathroom door.

Hunter shrugged, and Monty went back to sorting.

"I'll take these shirts and pants to be cleaned and pressed, and I'm putting all this back in the hamper. I'll run some loads in the morning for you, but you have to fold your own clothes and put them away because there are limits to this job, and handling your drawers is just about it."

"I thought I was the boss here?" Hunter growled more harshly than he intended.

"Job or no job, taking care of these"—he held up a pair of boxers by his fingertips—"is definitely outside my job description." He let them fall back into the hamper. "I bet those have ripened in there for two weeks. What do you do, wear them once and just buy more?" Monty scooped up the pants and shirts, and carried the armload out of the room, heading for the stairs without looking at him.

"I am the boss, you know," Hunter said from behind him.

"Fine. Then next time you can make sure the pictures of Mr. Happy and the Happettes don't make it all over the Internet." Monty shook his head and continued down the stairs without turning back as Hunter followed him. He dropped the laundry in the hallway before heading into the storeroom, then returned with a black trash bag. He shoved the clothes in it and then went into the kitchen. Water ran and stopped. When Monty returned, he had a wrapped plate of cookies that he handed to him. "You need to go or you'll be late," Monty said much more quietly, and then he went into the office once again. "I need to finish this up for you before I go."

31

Hunter peered into the office. Monty was head-down behind the computer, typing away. He stopped and the old printer in the corner began to work. Hunter hadn't used it in years—he'd thought it was dead and had been about to throw it out along with the rest of the ancient computer system he rarely used. Monty set the printed page in the center of the desk, put his things in his bag, and snatched up the laundry before leaving the house with Hunter following.

"I'll see you tomorrow," Monty said as he got into his old car, which looked as though it was on its last legs, and drove away while Hunter started for his party.

"YOUR NEW assistant made these?" Mark Henshaw asked as he gobbled down his second cookie.

"Yeah, but…," Hunter started.

"What? Charlene never bakes like this for me. Would he give my wife lessons?" Mark finished the cookie and grabbed yet another. "Raise you ten." He tossed a chip into the center of the table. "And he made these on his first day? It sounds to me like you hit the assistant jackpot." He leaned back in his chair.

"Man, how would you like some stranger knowing all your business all the time? He's already friends or something with Helen. She's sending him computers and phones and shit. Call." He threw a chip into the pot. "The guy knows nothing about football. He asked who I was playing poker with."

"Did you tell him?" Randall Barker asked.

"Yeah. He looked at me completely blank. Didn't register at all. No clue." Hunter waited for his turn and ended up folding because his cards went from bad to worse.

"So the guy doesn't know football—he knows *food*," Mark said.

"And all you care about is your belly," Clyde Haskins quipped before calling the hand, showing his cards, and raking in the pot. "If you paid more attention to the game, you'd know I was going to smoke your ass."

"You got to give the guy credit for one thing," Randall said. "He got you here on time, and that's like performing a miracle."

"I'm not that bad," Hunter said.

"Dude." Clyde leaned over the table. "You are late for everything. Coach was talking about it last season, and you know that's really bad. This is the first game we've started on time in a year. You're always half an hour late at least."

"Gives us more time for the beer," Mark said, and the guys all laughed. "Let this guy help you instead of fighting him." He shuffled and dealt the next hand.

The conversation quieted and they bet. Then Mark asked for cards, and Hunter bet when his turn came. It soon came down to him and Clyde, who called him.

"Full house, eights over aces," Clyde crowed.

"Four threes," Hunter said with delight and pulled in the biggest pot of the night so far. "Are you guys doing the charity calendar shoot?"

"Yeah," Mark said. "My wife thought it would be a good idea."

"Check the pictures when you're done and make sure any that show a little much are deleted, if you know what I mean."

"Are you kidding? Charlene has already said she was going to be there to watch everything like a hawk. That woman isn't going to let anything that she considers hers out on the Internet or anywhere else." He laughed. Clearly he liked that his wife cared about his image. "I take it you had a problem."

"Yeah. I thought Monty and the photographer were going to come to blows." He had to admit Monty fighting for his best interests was rather hot, and the man looked sexy when he was angry. "Monty is maybe five six and slight. The photographer was a good eight inches taller, but Monty stared him down and wasn't going to let it go."

"Sounds to me like you're whining over nothing. Monty was looking out for you." Randall dealt the cards. "Give the guy a break. You remember what it felt like to be the new guy. It's hard to fit in anywhere. So he doesn't know anything about football or who we are—"

"Dude," Mark interjected. "I love being recognized."

"Because you get free shit, you cheapskate," Joe chimed in. "Randall's right. So he doesn't know who you are or who any of us are. Do you want a guy as your assistant because you're famous and he wants to get close to you, or someone who treats you like anyone else and has your best interests at heart?" Joe slapped Mark's hand. "Leave some of the cookies for the rest of us." He snatched one as Mark took one more. That man could eat like nobody's business.

"Does Charlene starve you?" Hunter asked as a joke.

"She has me on a 'no junk food' diet," Mark said with a mouthful of cookie and grinned. The diet was clearly a lost cause. Off-season, Mark had a tendency to overeat. "Does this look like it needs to diet?" He stood up, patting his flat stomach. "Sometimes I think that woman is crazy. I like my ribs and sauce. Lord knows I work it off, if you know what I mean."

"No going there," Joe chided. "Or else Hunter will, and none of us needs to hear about that."

"Ain't nothing to go on about." Hunter threw his ante in the pot and concentrated on his cards.

"Dude…." Mark groaned. "How… you… I see guys looking at you all the time. Even straight ones. So go out and get you some. Just don't tell us about it." He grinned, his white teeth sparkling against caramel skin. Mark was drop-dead handsome, and Charlene kept him on the shortest leash imaginable. And for good reason. Mark had lots of chances, but word had it that Charlene made sure her man was more than happy to get what he needed at home. Besides, Hunter knew if Mark tried anything with anyone, he'd be singing soprano in two seconds.

After Hunter won another hand, they took a break for sandwiches and to watch some game tape. They all had to scout out the competition, and it was definitely more fun when they were together. After a few hours, they played some more poker, and then the evening broke up. Hunter got home around midnight, changed out of his dirty clothes, and fell into bed, worn out. But damn it all if he didn't spend the entire fucking night dreaming about a certain assistant with warm brown eyes and a butt that didn't quit.

Hunter woke in the early morning hours, got some water, and tried like hell to get the images of Monty out of his head. This was not going to do. He was not going to fantasize about his assistant. Their relationship was going to be professional and that was all. No matter how many times he woke up hard as nails just from thinking about him.

CHAPTER 4

His phone rang next to his bed. He groaned and snatched it off the nightstand. "Hello."

"Monty."

"Hunter?" He cracked his eyes open to look at the clock. "It's five thirty in the morning." He groaned and rolled over. "What's wrong?" He pushed back the covers and sat up.

"Yeah. It's five thirty. I thought you said you were a runner. I'm up and will be going for a run...."

"Okay," Monty said. "Let me pry my eyes open, and I'll be there when I can." He hung up the phone and tried to get to his feet but fell back on the bed. It was five fricking thirty in the morning. What in the hell was Hunter doing up so early? He should be asleep like a normal person. Monty scratched his butt as he left his room and padded to the bathroom, where he took one look in the mirror and groaned loudly. He washed his face and hair before styling it and making sure he wasn't a complete mess. After returning to his room and dressing, he went into the kitchen in search of coffee.

"What are you doing up?" Camille asked as she set her coffee mug down on the table. She was already dressed for her commute into work.

"My boss called. He wants to go for a run. Like I have anything to wear for that." He spun around. "Do I look like a gym bunny?" He poured coffee. "The man is rude and demanding as hell. I stopped his bits from getting all over the Internet by that sleazeball photographer, and does he say thank you? Nope. I even baked him cookies for his poker thingy and helped him with his laundry. God, I swear...."

"It's a job, so don't whine about it. You're his assistant, and that means you look out for him and do whatever he needs. It's generally a thankless job." Camille finished her coffee. "Who is this guy anyway? You said he was Mr. Davis, but that was all."

"Hunter...," Monty said.

"Hunter Davis, the football player? You're working for him?" Camille practically squealed. "He's an awesome player. You should see the way he uses his hands to snatch that ball out of the air. It's amazing, like he and the ball are one."

"What's all the noise?" Em asked as she joined them, still half-asleep.

"Your brother is Hunter Davis's assistant."

"I told you his name," Monty said.

"No. You came home last night, grumped about having to sort his laundry and drop it off at the cleaners, ate something, and then fell into bed. I didn't hear anything about Hunter Davis. Damn...." It seemed Monty had just made Camille's day.

"Wait a minute, you know football?"

"Yeah. I had four older brothers. Football was a staple in my house. Why?"

"You have to teach me about that stuff. He keeps throwing in my face that I don't know anything. So I thought I should learn something about it. Most of the players look good in those tight pants, but other than that...."

"Honey, I have to go." Camille put her mug in the sink, kissed Em, and headed for the door. "I'll talk you through the basics of football, I promise. For now, go out and get a jersey. At least it will show that you listened to him." The door closed behind her, and Monty got his bag.

"It's going to be all right," Em told him.

"I don't know. He's.... It's like working for a Greek god. The man is gorgeous, and twice yesterday I saw him with his shirt off. And I saw pictures of everything."

"Monty...."

"Let me just say that, *damn*, he's fine all over." Monty giggled, and Em shook her head. "I know I need to keep it professional and all, and I will. He's not my type anyway."

"Greek god isn't your type? Since when?" Em left the kitchen.

"It's the arrogant pain-in-the-ass part that isn't so attractive," Monty called after her.

"Yeah. You hate the pain-in-the-ass part. Right… I don't believe that, bottom boy," she called back, and Monty would have retorted, but he had to get going or he wasn't going to get to Hunter's on time.

"I THOUGHT you said you ran?" Hunter asked as he raced ahead momentarily.

"I did in college," Monty said as he zoomed past once more. "But you're the athlete. I'm just the assistant." He smiled and turned around the bike he was riding. He'd found it in Hunter's garage. Monty wasn't stupid enough to think he could ever keep up on foot with anyone in Hunter's physical condition. He turned again and came up behind Hunter, slowing his speed so he stayed with him.

"Why do you want me with you?" Monty asked. "I could be back finishing up your schedule." At least he'd been able to get a load of laundry into the machine and had Febrezed the bathroom before they left.

"What's my schedule for today?" Hunter asked, ignoring Monty's question.

"I printed it out for you and left it on the desk last night." He was already getting tired while Hunter was still going strong. "You have a meeting at eleven at your agent's to go over a deal. A team meeting this afternoon at two at the stadium, and then you're scheduled to have dinner at your coach's house. I added a note to your schedule tomorrow that we need to go shopping. Your morning was free, so I thought that would be a good time." Hunter groaned but didn't say no, which Monty thought was progress. "Is there anything I'm missing or that you want me to do?"

Hunter continued running but remained quiet. "There's something that I can't remember."

"I have everything from your agent and publicist on the schedule already, as well as the team. Is there someone else I need to talk to?" Monty was getting winded, but he continued on.

"I'll think of it." Hunter stopped, and Monty was grateful they seemed to be coming to the end of this ordeal. Then he continued running, and Monty groaned but kept up with him.

By the time they got back to the house, Monty could barely stand, and his ass hurt and so not in a good way. He put the bicycle away and waddled into the house. His legs ached as well as the rest of him. Of course Hunter was already upstairs taking a shower, so Monty used one of the downstairs bathrooms to clean up and change out of his sweaty clothes, which he put in the trunk of his car.

"I'm off to go shopping," he called and left the house. Hunter desperately needed groceries.

He returned an hour later, carrying the bags inside as Hunter barreled down the stairs. "Where were you?"

Monty lifted the bags higher and continued through to the kitchen, where he began putting the groceries away. "You could have called or texted me if you needed something." Monty wondered what this drama was all about.

"I have to go to this meeting, and Garvin said I was to look professional, but I don't know what that means. Should I wear a suit? This is a huge endorsement deal."

"Then let's find you something decent to wear." Monty got the last of the groceries put away and headed up the stairs. Of course Hunter had very little that would work. "Are they hiring Hunter the naked guy on a calendar or Davis, the sports star?"

"What?" Hunter snapped.

Monty paused. "I didn't mean to make you mad. What image are they hiring? If they want the sports celebrity, then I'd say wear some nice jeans and a jersey. That reminds them what you do and that you're good at it. If they're hiring the man who can model like you did yesterday...." Monty continued searching through the closet and came up with a pair of black slacks. "Wear these with this shirt and find a pair of dress shoes."

"I have some in the bottom of the closet."

Monty started hunting them up while Hunter changed behind him. Monty gave him time and tried not to peek, but he did just in time to see Hunter's ass disappear into his slacks. The man looked good in clothes, that was for certain. Now if Monty could only get him in the *right* clothes. He found the shoes and turned as Hunter put on his shirt.

"The buttons are wrong." Monty batted his hands away and corrected the buttons, his fingers occasionally brushing Hunter's warm, smooth skin.

"Thank you," Hunter said softly, and Monty looked up from what he was doing, meeting Hunter's intense gaze. He stopped, lost in his eyes for a few seconds. Damn, he was beautiful. Heat rose from inside him, and Monty parted his lips. Hunter stared at him, sending jolts of electricity through Monty with the strength of a high-voltage wire.

"You're welcome," Monty said without moving his hands. They felt so good against Hunter, and he slid them slightly, his knuckles skimming along his chest. Monty held still for a few seconds and then remembered where he was and what he was doing. He broke the gaze and finished buttoning Hunter's shirt. "That looks better. Leave two buttons open. Let them get a glimpse of your power."

"Excuse me?"

"Don't tell me you don't know what you have?" Monty took a step back. "Look, straight guys will never tell you this because they'll say they don't notice, but that's bullshit. You and your agent are going to negotiate, right? So you want to come in from strength, and yours is in your body. So let them see some of it. The shirt is a little tight, so it hugs your arms when you move. Your chest is a source of power, so show them a little. If they ask you to take off your shirt, then they're perving, so refer them to Garvin, who should have pictures."

"How do you know all this?"

"I'm a gay man who's used to having half-naked guys sell me everything on television and in magazines. It works, but what's even sexier and more erotic is the picture that only gives a sample, that leaves something out. You're giving them a sample and no more." Monty nodded. "You look really good, and tomorrow we'll get you more clothes like this. You're going to need them."

Actually, Monty thought Hunter looked edible, completely and totally delicious, but that particular ice-cream sundae was not on his menu. Hunter was his boss and things needed to stay that way. Monty needed to eat, and the fastest way to the unemployment line was to get involved with his employer. Well, the second fastest. The fastest was to turn the boss down, and he'd already been there.

"Go knock 'em dead." Monty followed Hunter down the stairs, going into the office to work while Hunter left through the garage.

God, he was tired. It was only ten thirty, but he swore he'd worked an entire day. Monty finally finished putting together Hunter's schedule for the next week and printed it in calendar form. He placed it on the kitchen counter so Hunter would be sure to see it at some point. Then Monty figured he might as well get the errands completed.

The doorbell rang as he was just getting ready to leave. "Yes?" he said to the older man standing on the front step. "Mr. Davis isn't home right now."

The man stepped forward. "Who the hell are you?"

"I'm his assistant. That's who the hell I am, and I'm sorry, but he isn't home, so you can call for an appointment or come back later. I expect him home at half past never." Monty pushed the door closed and threw the lock. He had no idea who this guy was, but Hunter had said that he wasn't to let anyone into the house.

Monty's phone rang, and he rushed to pick it up.

"What's going on, and why is my father standing outside my house?"

"Your dad?" Monty asked and stifled a groan. "You said… you practically yelled at me yesterday about…." Oh God, the hammer was about to fall.

"You can let him in and find out what he wants." Hunter hung up, and Monty went back to the front door and opened it.

"Sorry, I—"

"Hunter didn't tell me his assistant was a real bulldog," he said very unflatteringly as he charged into the house like the bulldog he was accusing Monty of acting like.

"What do you want? Hunter isn't here." Monty closed the door. "I have work to do."

"I guess we need to be introduced. I'm Simon Davis, Hunter's father."

"Monty Willis, Hunter's assistant." He still wasn't sure if he should approach him or not, but Simon held out his hand so Monty shook it. "Hunter said I wasn't to let anyone in."

"And I should have told you who I was," Simon explained. "So you're his new assistant. He didn't say he'd hired one, but I'm glad he did. He needs someone to take care of the daily tasks so he can work on what's important." Monty waited to hear what that was. "Football, son."

"I understand. Was there something you stopped by for?" He'd already told Simon that Hunter wasn't home.

"No. I was just getting out of the house and thought I'd come over here to hang out and watch some television." He went into the living room and flopped onto the sofa. "Say, would you bring me a sandwich or something?" Monty rolled his eyes and wanted to flip him off, but left the room and threw together a sandwich, and then he went to the laundry room, changed the loads, and gathered the things he needed.

"Here you are. Please lock up when you leave. I have some errands I need to run." Monty hurried to the door and got out of the house as quickly as he could. He set his bag on the floor of the backseat, prayed Lizzie would start, and took off down the drive. He had cleaning to pick up, and he wanted to stop off at a coffee roaster to get some decent coffee—what Hunter had was crap. Monty also had calls to make. He could have done that from the house, but with Simon there, thinking he was some kind of servant, it was best to make them from the coffee shop.

Hunter messaged as Monty was getting the coffee. *Where r u?*

Monty answered: *Running errands.*

Is dad @house?

He was when I left. Monty sat down, about to make the calls he needed to get someone to open the pool and for various other things.

Grrrr! Hunter sent, and Monty wasn't sure what he was supposed to do with that. He waited for another message, but none came, so he got to work.

Monty was able to find someone willing to come right out to check the spa and to open the pool. They said they'd be at the house in an hour, so Monty gathered up everything, carried it to the car, and drove back to the house. The driveway was full of cars, so he parked on the street, and when he came in, the television was on full blast and the living room was filled with guys Simon's age.

Hunter was going to kill him. Monty wondered how he was going to get these men out of here before Hunter got home. He returned to his car, grabbed the laundry, and hauled it upstairs.

"Mr. Assistant," Simon called as he reached the bottom of the stairs again. "We could all use something to eat and maybe some beer. If there's none in the house, why don't you run out and get us some?"

Monty went into the kitchen and wondered if some sort of bomb had gone off. Lunchmeat, bread, even the chicken wings he'd bought to make for Hunter in the next few days sat on the counter. Thankfully they were still really cold, so he put them away along with the rest of what could be salvaged. The other stuff he threw away and went about trying to clean up. Once the kitchen was under control, he got the last of the things out of the car. A cry went up as he passed through the hall and kept going into the kitchen to store what he'd gotten.

R U on your way to your meeting at the stadium? he texted to Hunter.

Leaving now was the response, and Monty put his phone in his pocket, then met the pool men and ushered them through the garage to the backyard. He wished more than anything that Simon and his pals would leave, but they seemed to be settling in for the duration.

"Where's that beer?" Simon asked when Monty came back inside.

"Don't have any," Monty said.

"Go get some," Simon barked, and Monty stormed into the living room.

"Go get your own beer, and while you're at it, have your party at your own house." He reached for the remote, but Simon snatched it and turned up the volume.

"This is my son's house," Simon told him.

One of the other men stood. "I'll go get some beer and snacks." He left to cheers from the rest of the assemblage.

Monty turned and left, seething. This was the rudest and most disrespectful behavior Monty had ever seen. Hunter deserved more respect than this. The washing machine beeped, and he went in to move the clothes to the dryer. He saw the gray panel on the wall and grinned. Monty pulled it open and hit the main breaker to the house. Suddenly the noise from the other room became as silent as the grave. He left the room and went into the kitchen to meet Simon.

"What the hell happened?"

Monty shrugged. "The power must be out." Simon moved toward the refrigerator, but Monty blocked him. "Don't open it or the cold will dissipate." He glared at Hunter's father and said nothing further.

"It'll come back on soon," Simon said, but the other men were getting restless.

"Let's go. The power is on at my house, and we can watch baseball there." The guys all stood, and they began to leave the house, groaning because the television wasn't nearly as big at whoever's house the group of slobs was headed to.

"Good to meet you, Simon," Monty said when everyone else was gone and he was about to leave. Simon grunted and pulled the door closed behind him. Monty locked the door, grabbed the kitchen trash can, and began cleaning up plates, glasses, and bits of sandwich and chips off the furniture. He had to remind himself that this wasn't his house, but he wasn't going to treat it any less than he would his own home, and these men certainly had.

Monty turned the power back on, turned off the loud television, found the vacuum and finished cleaning up, wiped down the tables, and then left the room. He finished up in the kitchen. He had to go back through and turn everything off, but at least the house was put back together.

The pool men had finished up: the spa was clean and no longer smelled yucky, and the pool was running and full, sparkling in the sun. Monty took the bill they presented, paid them out of his own meager funds, and sent them on their way. He figured he'd find out how to get reimbursed later. He'd have to ask Hunter about that.

Monty ended up going back to the grocery store to replace what had been scarfed down by the geezers and arrived back at the house just after Hunter, pulling in right behind his car.

"Where is everyone?" Hunter asked. "They usually stay all afternoon, until their wives start to call them home." He unlocked the door, and Monty followed him inside, carrying the bags. He said nothing and went into the kitchen, letting Hunter do what he needed to. "I thought you said my dad was here. Where's the mess and the crap they always leave?"

"Oh, they left plenty of that. I cleaned it up once they left after the power outage." He continued putting away the groceries and gave no further explanation. "Do they come over often?"

"Every Thursday like clockwork. It's their thing, and I have to put up with it."

"Why?" Monty asked and chastised himself yet again for opening his mouth.

"He's my dad."

"And he shows you no respect." Monty took care of the last of the groceries and went into the office. He returned with a piece of paper that he handed to Hunter.

"What's this?"

"A request for every Thursday off for the rest of my probationary period. I'm your assistant, not your maid, and I certainly am not your father's 'bring me a sandwich and some beer' boy. I said I'd do my best for you and I will, but I'm not going to fetch and carry beers and cater drunken-old-guy afternoons away from their wives where they act like slobs and disrespect you in your own house. That I can't do. I'll treat your home as well or better than I treat my own." He hoped he was getting his point across.

Hunter remained silent, slowly folding the paper and then handing it back.

"I also had some expenses."

"Let me know what they are and I'll make sure you're reimbursed, then set up something so you have access to funds in the future."

"How did your meetings go? If you don't mind my asking." Monty figured it was best if he changed the subject.

He handed Monty a separate sheet of paper, and Monty opened it, looked at the scribbles, and tried not to react. "We came to a deal and set up the initial schedule. I have to go to New York next Monday, so I'll need a hotel room for Sunday and Monday. I'll also need you to go with me. So make train and hotel reservations. There are also details on the schedule while we're there." Hunter went into the kitchen, and Monty stared at the scrap of paper, wondering how he could make anything out of it. Things had been going so well so far. He was usually fine if he took his time, but with this the lettering seemed all over the place, and he set the page aside.

In the end he called Helen, who passed on all the information he needed, and he updated Hunter's schedule. She had already rescheduled some of his conflicts, so Monty made those changes as well and jotted down a note to call Hunter's publicist to reschedule the others.

"For the trip to New York, I've arranged a limousine to pick you up. And I booked a suite at the Plaza for your stay. Garvin will be there as well. You'll need to bring all your equipment with you and stay with Hunter while he's there. Things have a tendency to change quickly, and he must be everywhere he's needed on time," Helen explained.

"I know."

"You're doing great so far."

"His father doesn't think so."

"What happened?" Helen asked, and Monty told her about not letting him in initially and then turning off the power to get him and his cronies to leave. Helen burst out laughing. "That was brilliant, absolutely brilliant."

"But what if Hunter gets mad?"

"What about me?" Monty lifted his gaze and saw Hunter standing in the doorway.

"Crap," Monty said. "I'll call you back." That was if he still had a job.

"You staged the power outage to get rid of my father?" Hunter stalked over to the desk, and Monty pushed the chair back, ready to make a run for it. This was not going to go well; he could feel it.

"Yes," he croaked.

"Damn, you're a devious one, aren't you?" Hunter continued glaring at him. "I only wish I'd thought of it." Then he smiled.

"You aren't angry?"

Hunter shook his head. "You looked after my home the way you would your own. I can't ask for more than that." Hunter sank down into one of the chairs on the other side of the desk. "Sometimes I think my dad likes the idea of having a football player as a son more than he actually likes me."

The ache in Hunter's voice and the hurt in his eyes made Monty want to help him and take that away, but there was nothing he could do. "What about next Thursday?"

"I'll tell him that the parties here have to stop." That wasn't going to be an easy conversation for Hunter.

"The pool people were here and the spa is heating up. The pool is still cold, but it's open, and once it warms up you can swim if you like." Monty thought it best to talk about business rather than Hunter's family, since the hurt he saw in Hunter's eyes was beyond his reach. "I also got your dry cleaning and hung it in your closet." He reprinted the adjusted calendar and handed it to Hunter. "This is your schedule for the next week. I added your morning runs."

"What's PT?" Hunter looked it over.

"Personal Time. I figured I'd try to blank out some time for you so you could work out or just hang if you liked. It's so easy to have every minute of every day scheduled and then you have nothing for yourself. So I was trying to prevent that."

"Okay." Hunter didn't move, and Monty wondered what he wanted. Eventually Hunter got up and left, so Monty went back to work.

Once he had everything done that he could think of, Monty went in search of Hunter and found him in the hot tub.

"If it's okay, I'm going to go home now." He was tired beyond belief. "You have to leave in less than an hour for your dinner with your coach."

Hunter stood, water sluicing down his impeccable body. Monty wanted to look and knew he needed to turn away, but Hunter was watching him, so he tried to concentrate on his face rather than the flesh on display. "I'm getting out now, and I'll get dressed to go."

"I put the clean laundry in your room and the towels and stuff are all put away. Unless there's something you need, I'll see you in the morning."

"Go on home." Hunter grabbed for his towel and rubbed himself down before slipping on a robe. "Yes, I'll see you in the morning, but it isn't necessary for you to come on my run with me. Eight o'clock or so should be fine."

"Okay." Monty turned and went back inside, got his things, and went out to his car—which refused to start. "Come on, Lizzie. This

48

isn't the time to die on me." He tried again and the starter clicked but did nothing else. He went back inside, wondering who to call.

"What's going on?" Hunter asked as he padded through the house, presumably on his way to his room.

"My car won't start. I'll call my sister or her partner and see if one of them can pick me up." Either that or he'd walk to the train station to get home.

"Here." Hunter picked up a set of keys from the bowl on the side table and handed them to Monty. "Take the BMW, and tomorrow you can arrange to have the car looked at. I'll take the Porsche to the coach's." Hunter climbed the stairs, and Monty stared after him.

CHAPTER 5

"I HATE shopping." Hunter sat in the passenger seat of his own car as Monty drove to the mall.

"King of Prussia is amazing, and we can find anything you need." Monty was obviously excited. "We'll park near Bloomingdale's. It's a great store where we can get the basics without spending all day going from store to store."

"If you say so." Hunter was more than a little worried. "Look, Monty, there's something I think you need to know. There's a reason that I have blue shirts and tan pants. It's because I know they go together, so…."

"You're color-blind," Monty said. "I figured that out when I saw your closet. No one needs that many blue shirts."

"Oh." He was surprised at how much Monty had divined about him.

"It's no problem. Once we get the new clothes, I'll sort your closet so you know what's where and we can work up outfits that will allow you to dress easily even if you don't know the color." Monty pulled into the parking lot and up to the valet. They got out, and he handed over the keys, took the ticket, and they headed inside. "I promise we'll make this as painless as possible."

"If you say so." Hunter followed Monty into the men's section of the store, and Monty wasted no time looking things over.

"We'll start with pants. These are dress slacks. They're lightweight." He handed them to Hunter. "Do you like the feel?"

"They're nice."

"Good. What's your waist? A thirty-one or so?" Monty looked him over and then picked a couple pairs of pants off the rack. "Go try these on. I want to check the size, and then we can go from there."

50

Hunter trudged off to do as Monty asked. He found a clerk who led him to a fitting room. The first pair of pants was too tight and a little too short, but the second pair felt perfect. He stepped out so Monty could see.

"Those look great on you." He fidgeted around him and then stepped back. "Good. Go take those off, and we'll finish looking around."

Hunter groaned and went back inside. This was totally stupid, and he was going to be here all day. Hunter got back into his regular clothes and came out with both pairs of pants to find Monty standing in front of him, his hands loaded with hangers.

"Here are three pairs of those pants in various shades. They look great on you, and the ones I got will go with blue, as well as with any of these." He held up what had to be a dozen shirts in various styles. "We can pick out some jeans if you like, and I got you some new casual pants so the old ones can be put out to pasture." He handed things over.

Monty was like a whirlwind. He got him belts and some new shoes as well as fresh socks because, as he put it, he was having trouble getting the stink out of the old ones.

"Is this all?"

"For now. With what you have at home, you should have a well-rounded wardrobe now. In a few months, we can get you some shorts, and you'll be all set for next summer. Is that cool?"

"Sure." With his arms full, Hunter walked to a checkout station. "But I don't understand the jersey. I don't need one of those."

"That's for me," Monty said, snatching it away. "It's going to be huge on me, but it's the smallest size they carry in the official stuff." Monty held it up. "Maybe I can cinch it or something."

Hunter nearly choked. "You don't cinch a football jersey." Hunter snatched the jersey away and set it aside. "Just stick to your regular clothes. You always look really good to me."

He piled the clothes at the checkout, and the lady began ringing them up. He didn't bat an eyelash when she announced that the total was nearly fifteen hundred dollars. He handed her his card, and she completed the sale and packaged everything neatly before handing them the purchases.

"Was that so bad?" Monty asked as they walked out of the store.

"I guess not." Hunter popped the trunk, and they set all the bags inside. "You aren't going to tell anyone about the color-blind thing, are you?"

"Of course not. That's not my secret to tell." Monty put in the last bag and tapped the trunk so it would automatically close and latch. "Not that it's anything to be ashamed of. But I will be sure to keep it in mind going forward." Monty got back into the car and drove them home. "I've been thinking. I could devise a code to put in the labels of your clothes. That way you'll always know what goes with what, even if the closet gets mixed up. Let me think on it."

Hunter was floored that Monty would take such care for him. He figured it came with being a good assistant, but it really was nice to be fussed over sometimes.

HUNTER WAS getting used to having Monty around, so on Saturday, when he wasn't at the house, Hunter didn't really know what to do. He watched television, but it seemed lame to sit home alone. During the week, when Hunter was at home, Monty was there to talk with, and it was nice to know someone else was in the house. Hunter had plans with Mark and Charlene for dinner, but most of the day he just worked out, napped, or sat around doing pretty much nothing. God, he hated being bored.

On Sunday, Monty arrived early, of course, and Hunter was ready with his bag that Monty had largely packed for him. Monty was still using Hunter's car because his had apparently died and was beyond saving.

"I'm going to get a new car as soon as we get back from New York," Monty said as he handed him the keys. "Though driving your car the last few days has spoiled me for what I'm going to be able to afford." Monty smiled nervously. "Thank you for letting me use it.

That was very kind of you." Monty began checking his phone. "The limousine should be here in just a few minutes."

"Limo?"

"Sorry. Helen arranged for a limousine to drive us instead of taking the train. We'll apparently have it at our disposal the entire time we're in New York, and we also have reservations at the Plaza. Garvin is going to be there as well. It's all taken care of." Monty peered out the window. "And here is the car. Do you need me to get the bags?"

"No. The driver can take care of that," Hunter told him. "It's Sunday, so sit back and relax a little, would you? We don't meet with anyone until tomorrow." Hunter rolled his suitcase out to the car, handed Monty's to the driver, and then climbed inside. "So just relax and enjoy the trip."

"But I'm working," Monty said as he settled on the seat.

"Not today. I know you don't know very much about football, but this is an off day. And one thing I've learned after years in sports is, when you get an off day, you make the most of it. So that's what we're going to do."

"I know there's the training camp and then the preseason where they try out new plays to see how things are working. Then after that there's the sixteen-game season and then postseason playoffs to the Super Bowl." Monty grinned. "I did some research, and my sister's girlfriend is a huge football and Red Hawks fan. She nearly flipped out when I told her I was working for you. I think she'd want to have your babies… if she wasn't a lesbian."

Hunter shot him a look as the car pulled forward.

"There's television, and you can have what you want to drink." Hunter opened a cooler and pulled out a bottle of champagne. "There's orange juice too." He grabbed two glasses, poured juice in each one, and then popped the bottle of champagne and added some to the glasses. "A breakfast drink."

"Did you have anything to eat?" Monty dug in his bag, then handed him a granola bar and took one for himself.

"What else do you have in there?"

Monty shrugged. "It's just my bag. What kind of assistant would I be if I wasn't prepared for everything I could think of? It's early, and I bet you went for a run, made some coffee, and then waited for me to make you some breakfast, only I wasn't there."

Hunter hated to admit Monty was right, especially with that knowing smirk on his face. He ate the granola bar and sat back as they rolled out of the city.

"Can I ask you something?" Monty sipped from his glass, and Hunter nodded. "Why is the color-blind thing such a big deal? Lots of guys have trouble seeing some sort of color."

"Uniforms are colored, and on the field we identify our teammates by the color of their uniform. If a guy is barreling down on you, it's important to know in an instant if he's someone working to block for you or a defender ready to mow you down. Most guys do that by the uniform. The color makes them instantly recognizable."

"I can see that. The field seems chaotic with everyone running around the way they do."

"It can be. But I learned to compensate for the color issue a long time ago." He sat forward. "See, the away team wears white and the home team wears their colors, so there's always a variation in light and dark. That I can see. So if we're away, I know my guys have light uniforms and the other team will have dark ones." Hunter stopped. "Color blindness doesn't mean I can't see color altogether, and it varies from person to person. I can see some color, but it isn't as vivid in most cases for me. Some guys can't differentiate between blue and yellow, while others are green and red. I have both to a degree. Most of the time, I don't even think about it, but with clothes it's really hard." Hunter paused and then figured he may as well go for broke.

"The kids at school…," Monty prompted and sipped from his glass.

"I remember asking Mom to let me dress myself. I looked fine to me, but the kids all made fun of me. I was eight and my dad had just signed me up for football, so when the kids started picking on me because of my clothes, my mom made sure to help me lay out my clothes and I got mad. Dad told me to put that anger into my football, so I did. As I played, I got bigger and I was good, so I got attention."

"But inside there was still the kid who was picked on because his clothes didn't match?" Monty added for him.

"Yeah. Kids can be mean. But I figured it out, at least until the kids started picking on me for wearing the same colors, but by then I was bigger than they were and I could intimidate them into silence." Hunter emptied his glass and made himself another drink.

"So you were a bully?"

"Not really. I was strong, and I could stand up for myself. By the time I was sixteen, I knew I was gay, and that only added to the things I felt I had to keep quiet. So I threw myself into football and said to hell with the rest of it. Sports were the only thing I was good at, and I managed to get a scholarship to play and was the star of the team. My mom and dad were proud of me, as were my coaches. I was flying high." The car pulled to a stop, and Hunter glanced out the window before turning back to Monty. "I came out at twenty, and most of my teammates were pretty cool. I had two stellar years and got drafted by the Red Hawks."

"Did you get grief because you were gay?"

"Shit, yes. Teams didn't want to draft me because they were afraid of team morale and all that crap. Like I was going to go trolling in the locker room or something. It was mostly management being dicks. They're a bunch of old farts who are way behind the times. Sure, I got a hard time from some of the other players, and there are a few who hold me at arm's length, but once I started making plays and we began to win, they backed off. We'll never be friends and all, but we respect each other, and that's what it's all about. They're my teammates, and I rely on them, and they rely on me."

"But what if they wouldn't have backed you up? Camille says that other gay players felt left out in the cold by their teams, or at least she said that was the perception."

55

"Coach is awesome and has my back." The limousine was huge, and Hunter changed seats so he could sit next to Monty. That way he wouldn't have to talk as loudly. "There was one player who really gave me grief. He didn't want anything to do with me." Hunter shrugged. "It was the way he was brought up. But I sought him out and talked with him. I explained how things were, and that if the team was to succeed, we needed to work together."

"Did it work?"

"I played poker with him the other night. He and I are close friends now, and Mark is an awesome man. Charlene, his wife, had a lot to do with helping him see that I was just another player. But it's a testament to him as a person that he was willing to look past what he thought in order to see the real me." Hunter took a deep breath when he realized just how much football had truly given to him.

"How did you manage that?"

"When we talked we found out we have something in common." Hunter wanted to empty his glass once again because he found himself getting way too close to a subject he didn't want to discuss. "Both he and I were picked on. Mark was a bussed-in kid, so he went to a nearly all-white high school, and he felt like an outsider too. In some ways I still do." He set his glass aside so he wouldn't be tempted to get a little toasty and ate another granola bar so there would be something in his stomach. Monty handed him another one, and he ate that as well.

"What about you? When did you realize you were gay?"

Monty giggled and put his hand in front of his mouth. "Look at me. It isn't as though being gay was any sort of secret. I'm small, talk like this, and walk the way I walk. I don't do affectations. I'm just me. So everyone knew I was gay by the time I was thirteen."

"God…." Hunter tried to imagine the abuse Monty must have suffered at school.

"I joined the gay/straight alliance and owned who I was. I was the out gay kid in eighth grade, and I was friends with all the girls. And since the boys were noticing them and I was in their groups, they left me alone because the girls would have turned on them in an instant."

"So you never did any sports?" Hunter asked. "I bet you'd be great at the strength and balance type sports."

"I tried out for track, but those uniforms...." Monty chuckled. "I liked to run, but I didn't fit in with any of those groups. But balls...." He grinned. "The only ones I'm good with are attached."

"I bet you are," Hunter said without thinking or, more accurately, said exactly what he was thinking, and then wanted to slap himself when he saw Monty's surprise. "Sorry, that was rude."

"I was good in gymnastics in gym class, but I wasn't going to try out for the team. Mostly I kept a low profile, studied as best I could, and then tried to get a job as soon as I graduated."

"You didn't go to college?"

"No. I'm not smart enough, and there was no way I could pay for it. See, you're color-blind, and I'm dyslexic. I had a hard-as-hell time in school, and no one figured it out until I was a senior. I had some help then, and I've learned to deal with it. So it's all good now. But college was never in the cards for me, unlike Em. But she's between jobs right now, so Camille is supporting her."

"They sound like good people."

"I don't think I could have survived the last year without them. They're wonderful, and I love them both. Growing up, it was just Em and me. Our mother worked and did her best, but she drove us both crazy because we had to do everything around the house. I used to come home every day from school to a list of chores. I resented her because the other kids got to have fun and go places, and to a degree I still do, but she did her best, I guess." Monty handed him his glass. "I think you better take this. I'm already getting maudlin, and if I have any more, I'll be telling you every sad story I have."

"A guy like you?" Hunter shook his head.

"Yeah. Being an out gay kid isn't all glamour and arranging flowers, you know." Monty cracked the joke, but Hunter got the idea that the humor was hiding deeper pain. He leaned forward, and

57

Monty turned to face him. Hunter sat back like he'd been slapped by the hurt in Monty's eyes. He'd seen that soul-deep hurt in the mirror, looking back at him. He knew what that felt like. Hunter wanted to ask what had happened to him, but then, he wasn't ready to talk about his own hurt, so he turned away and briefly closed his eyes.

"I went over the schedule with Helen late on Friday. We're supposed to meet with the clients tomorrow morning for breakfast. It's to get to know the team of people you'll be working with. After that, you're going to their office to go through the final contract with them and Garvin. It's supposed to be a formality, but watch for curveballs. That's when they'll throw them in."

"Don't you ever take a break from work?" Hunter asked.

"Let's go over this, and then I promise I'll relax. As I was saying, the curveballs will come in the contract review."

"Is that what Garvin thinks?"

"I only talked to Helen, but that's what I think. It's what they do in the movies." Damn, Monty could make him smile. "After that, there's a dinner with the team from Johnston. Helen said it will be big because they want to show you off to their people. On Tuesday morning, provided all the contract stuff goes well, you'll meet with the photographer and then have your first photo session. Let's hope this guy is less creepy than the last one." Monty had his phone in hand. "What sessions do you want me in?"

"All of them," Hunter said. "There may be some parts of the contract review that are confidential and you'll probably need to step out, but I'm going to need your support. These things take all my attention, and something always comes up, and I can't be in two places at once."

"But...." Monty was clearly shocked. "I haven't worked for you that long and—"

"You said you'd do your best for me and that I could trust you to keep things to yourself. So that's what I'm doing." He trusted Monty. He hadn't realized how much he was going on that instinct until Monty questioned it. "Is there a reason I shouldn't?"

Monty colored and shook his head. "I wanted you to be sure."

And just like that, Hunter realized the kind of man Monty was. Unless he was a great actor, which Hunter doubted since Monty tended to wear his heart on his sleeve, Monty was straightforward and a square shooter. And to think he'd almost not given him the job. "I am."

"We'll have the limousine to use in New York so we aren't going to have to take taxis and stuff. Are there any reservations you want me to make or clubs that you want to visit?" Monty asked.

He hadn't been to a club in years. "See if you can find a place where we can have some fun after the dinner thing. It might be interesting. But no reservations. We'll show up, and I can probably get us in if the men at the curb are sports fans."

"Okay. Is there anything else I can do?"

"Not for today." Hunter took Monty's phone and set it aside. "Relax and take it easy for a while. We'll get to the city in an hour or so, and after that it will take even more time to navigate to the hotel." Hunter sat back and took his own advice. Monty seemed to as well.

They rode along at a steady speed, Hunter watching out the window. Half an hour out of the city, Monty seemed to doze off, and with the rocking of the road, he shifted to the side and leaned against Hunter. Monty must be comfortable. He smacked his lips a few times and pressed closer. Hunter put an arm around him and let him sleep. They had full days ahead of them, and rest was going to be important.

Of course Hunter couldn't rest for a second. Monty slept on and his scent filled the car. Hunter found he spent most of his time watching Monty. His eyes fluttered a few times, and his lips pursed and unpursed. Hunter wondered if Monty was dreaming he was kissing someone. Was Monty thinking about him? The thought sent a jolt of attraction through him, and Hunter realized he liked the thought of Monty picturing him. Hunter had dreamed of Monty more nights than he wanted to admit to.

Monty was adorable. Hunter had always pictured himself with another player or someone his same size. Big and strong. Monty was none of that, but Hunter was fascinated. Maybe it was his big "take no prisoners" mentality. He'd run the risk of incurring Hunter's wrath to get his father out of the house just because he thought his dad and his friends weren't respecting him. Hunter had never thought of it that way, but Monty had been right. His dad was taking advantage and treating him and his home badly. Hunter still had to deal with that, but thought maybe he'd let Monty at his dad. He'd like to see that matchup, and he had little doubt Monty would win.

"Who knew so much could come in a small package?" Hunter whispered to himself.

Monty shifted slightly on the seat but didn't wake up. They were approaching the city, and Hunter wasn't sure if Monty had been here before, so he gently shook his shoulder.

"Sleepyhead," he teased, and Monty slowly sat up. "Do you want to see the city?"

Monty's brown eyes slid open, and he jumped back. "Sorry." His cheeks darkened dramatically and he checked himself over. "I didn't mean to use you as a pillow. I guess I was tired and...."

Hunter pointed out the window to give Monty some time to recover from his blush, as well as the prominent bulge in his pants. Whatever Monty had been dreaming about, it certainly seemed good. "We're coming into the city, and I thought you might want to look. Have you been here before?"

"Yes. On a high-school French club trip. We came up here and spent some time in the various ethnic neighborhoods so we could get a feel for how people brought their cultures with them when they immigrated."

"Sounds interesting," Hunter deadpanned.

"It was really an excuse to eat lots of food and see stuff. We went to the top of the Empire State Building and took a trip to Ellis Island and the Statue of Liberty. Things like that. It was fun, but we only had a few days. I wish we'd been able to see a show, but that wasn't in the budget." Monty barely sat still as they got closer to the city. He bounded from one side of the limousine to the other so he could see what he wanted.

Of course, as they got closer, the city view disappeared. It didn't take too long before they were through the tunnel, coming out on the other side and entering Manhattan's stop-and-go traffic.

Monty was so cute, craning his head so he could see the tops of the buildings as they passed. "I think we're here," Monty said after the car rolled to a stop and the driver opened their door.

"The Plaza."

Monty jumped out, and Hunter followed. A bellman took their bags and trailed after them into the hotel, where Hunter checked them in. The bellman rode with them to their floor and escorted them to their room, which was nice with two bedrooms and a living area between.

"What do you want to do first?" Monty asked as he carried Hunter's bag into the bigger bedroom and began unpacking it, hanging up the clothes in the closet.

Hunter pushed the curtains open the entire way and stared down at the park. "I thought we'd find a sporting-goods store and go to the park for a while." Hunter turned as Monty pulled the last items out of the bag. "The second jersey is for you," Hunter said. "That one."

Monty held it up.

"It's an official one. As in it's been played in. Go unpack and put it on. We'll get some lunch, and then I'll teach you a little about football."

"You're serious?"

"Yeah. We have all day, and it's gorgeous out, so we can play in every New Yorker's backyard."

Monty lowered the jersey. "You know I can't catch anything except the flu. You saw me with the keys."

"It'll be fine. We'll have some fun. That's what the game is really all about. I know there's a lot of money involved and sponsors and crap like that. But football is a game, and it's supposed to be enjoyed. Since you never played, let me show you some of the fun."

"Okay. It's your funeral." Monty sounded down, but Hunter noticed the way he held the jersey to his chest. Hunter was thrilled Monty liked his gift. Once Monty had left, Hunter changed into jeans and his jersey. Then he put on comfortable shoes and waited for Monty in the living area.

"This place is big enough to get lost in," Monty said and came out of the bedroom with his jersey on backward. Hunter wondered how he'd done that. He walked over and tapped Monty on the shoulder. Shaking his head, he tugged off the shirt and turned it around. Hunter got his first look at a shirtless Monty, and damn, he was pretty. He wasn't bulky by any means, but there wasn't a lick of fat on him anywhere.

"I'm super skinny." Monty grabbed for the shirt, but Hunter stopped him, smoothing his hands down his shoulders.

"No. You're perfect." He held Monty's gaze, seeing him blush and doing the same himself. Hunter cleared his throat. "You should put a light T-shirt on and the jersey over it."

"Okay," Monty said, without looking away, blinking those huge-lashed eyes at him. Hunter leaned forward, drawn by Monty's parted lips, gorgeous eyes, and the sight of skin and the scent of musk. He was hard enough to pound nails, and damn if he didn't want Monty... bad. His mouth went dry, and he was actually contemplating how his lips would taste and the sounds he'd make when Hunter took him in his arms, held him tight, pressing what was certainly smooth, warm skin to his. Fuck, he wanted to find out how that little butt he'd seen swinging back and forth like a damn metronome every time Monty went up the stairs would feel in his hands.

"Okay?" Hunter asked, mostly repeating what Monty had said, because his brain had nearly shut down.

"Okay. I should put on a T-shirt." Monty took the jersey and held it in front of his chest like a shield, before turning and entering the bedroom.

Hunter watched him go, berating himself for hesitating. He took what he wanted on the field, so why hadn't he just done the same now? Of course, there was only one answer—Michael.

Hunter pushed that from his mind and told his errant body to calm down. If he had time, he'd go to his room and jack off to relieve the pressure. But then again, since he was most likely to do that thinking about Monty, it wasn't likely to help the situation very much. Hunter had fantasized about men for years, but he tried not to think about guys he knew. That always seemed like an invasion somehow. But the last week or so, he hadn't been able to stop his imagination from conjuring up Monty in all kinds of situations. In the end he went to the bathroom and splashed some water on his face, and when he returned, Monty was waiting for him.

Monty made sure they each had a key to the room, and he checked his e-mail one last time before they left the room.

"Where do you want to eat?" Monty asked as they stepped out the front door of the hotel and onto the streets of New York.

The excitement of the city always made Hunter's heart race. He loved this place, with its energy and vitality. He thought that someday he might want to move here, but even on his salary, that would be daunting. "There are places everywhere."

"True. But you need to be careful. Getting sick or something because you ate a hot-dog-cart hot dog is not going to look very good."

"Okay. How about there?" Hunter pointed.

"No TGI's or Olive Garden. This is New York." Monty walked down the street until a restaurant caught his eye. He waved to the sign. "How about Italian?"

"Sounds good."

They went inside and had pasta with pesto, Caesar salad, and a glass of wine each, and came out stuffed to the gills.

"There's a toy store. I bet we can get what we need there." Hunter took off across the street and grabbed a football from a display. He waited in line, paid, and went back outside to join Monty, who was still looking all around. "Let's go."

"If we must," Monty said, and they crossed the street and plunged into Central Park with its rambling walks, canopy of trees, bridges, zoo, and every other diversion a park could offer.

"This is perfect," Hunter said when they came to an area of lawn surrounded by trees. People sat on blankets around the edges, but Hunter jogged to the middle and handed Monty the ball. "A football is different because of the shape. Grip it like this." He positioned Monty's fingers. "Look where you want to throw and pretend you're dancing with it. The movement is fluid. See? Let the ball go like this to send it on its way."

"That's a weird way of putting it."

"In football, accuracy is everything. Passes get completed or are intercepted based on it."

Hunter stepped away, and Monty threw him the ball. Well, he threw it, anyway, right onto the ground. He scrambled to pick it up and tried again. This time he overcompensated and threw it high in the air. Hunter jumped and caught it, throwing a spiral straight back to Monty, who caught it.

"Good job."

"Is this what you do?" Monty tried throwing again and did better.

"You're getting it." Hunter threw the ball back, and Monty jumped out of the way. "The ball isn't going to hurt you. I won't throw hard."

"Too many years of killer dodgeball." Monty was most likely trying to be flip, but Hunter knew the truth of it. He'd been one of the kids who had thrown the ball as hard as he could. He was a jock, and a display of power was always expected if he would be able to keep up the appearances he needed to with his peers.

"I promise I won't hurt you. Now throw it back."

Monty picked up the ball and threw it over his head. Hunter jumped and missed. A man from behind him caught it and sent him back a perfect spiral.

"Thanks."

"We're putting together a pickup game," the man said.

Under normal circumstances Hunter might have joined for fun, but not with Monty. "Not today. Thanks," Hunter called back.

"You don't have to worry about how good you are or anything," the guy added, and Monty snickered behind his hand. "It's just some guys from my college team. We're going to mess around and we're a man short. After all, if you're Red Hawks fans, you have to have guts to show yourselves in New York."

"Young man," Monty said with a snicker. "Do you know who this is? The jersey, it's his, as in his team, his number, and his name. Hunter is showing me the basics of football. Actually, I think he's taking pity on a guy who can't catch anything."

"You're Hunter Davis? Really? I'm such a goof. But yeah, you're welcome to join us. That would be so cool."

"Like I said, another time would be awesome. Thanks, though." Hunter shook the kid's hand, and he hurried back to join his friends.

"You could have played if you wanted."

"No, I can't. There are tons of rules, and once the game got started, I'd end up playing full charge because it's who I am, and someone could get hurt. Football is all testosterone, and once it gets going, it's hard to dial it back." Hunter threw Monty the ball and he caught it. "See, you're getting it."

"But what about the other parts, like the tackling and the part where you stare at each other's butts? That's my personal favorite."

"I bet it is," Hunter quipped. "There are lots of rules. You get four downs to make ten yards, either rushing on the ground or by passing. If you get the ball past the other team's goal, it's a touchdown and six points. The important thing is to have some fun." Hunter caught Monty's throw and raced toward him. Monty squeaked and got out of the way, tripped over his own feet and sprawled on the ground.

"What was that for?" Monty asked as he brushed himself off.

"I was going for a touchdown," Hunter answered as though it were obvious.

"You scared me." Monty turned to look behind him. "I'm checking my underwear."

Hunter had to laugh. "Drama queen. How about I toss the ball, you catch it, and try to run past me."

"Sure. Like that's going to happen." Monty got into position, and Hunter threw. Monty caught the ball and ran forward, dodging to the side at the last second. Hunter lunged for him and caught Monty around the waist, tackling him to the ground as gently as he could. Monty smacked him on the shoulder.

"What was that for?" Hunter asked, pinning Monty to the ground.

"Duh.... Getting me dirty." Monty lay still, and Hunter stared into his eyes, neither of them moving. "Though I can forgive you if you tell me I don't have to wash your real uniforms."

"Nope." Hunter loved the bright smile on Monty's lips.

"Are you going to let me up?"

"I'm thinking I like the view from right here and want to look a little while longer." He could get lost in those eyes and never get away. "Sorry." Hunter stood up and offered his hand to Monty.

The college kids approached from where they'd been playing.

"Could we get your autograph?" asked the guy who had invited him to play.

"If you get a marker, I'll sign this football to you," Hunter said. He figured they were done. One of the guys ran to his backpack and returned with a Sharpie. Hunter signed and dated the ball and handed it over. "Have fun, guys."

"Thanks!" they all said and shook his hand before taking their prize, chattering the entire time.

"You made their day," Monty said.

Hunter nodded and turned back to Monty. "Let's go for a walk. There's plenty to see, and we have all afternoon. Where do you want to go?"

Monty shrugged, so Hunter led them farther into the park. They came upon an RC boat pond, and Hunter rented a boat and handed the control to Monty, who laughed wildly as he propelled it around the pond, avoiding the other boats.

"I always wanted one of these. There was a park with a pond near our house in Lancaster. One of the other kids had a boat that he and his dad built, and they used to run it on the pond for hours. Of course, I never got to play with it… until today." Monty played, laughed, and vibrated with excitement for the entire half hour and then turned in the boat with a gleam in his eye that was worth so much more than money. "What's next, oh tour guide of magic?"

"Come on." Hunter grinned as they walked deeper into the park to the lake, and he rented a paddleboat. Monty and he got in, and they pedaled around the lake and under one of the bridges. Monty took pictures with his phone, snapping the scenery around them. Hunter used his longer arms to get a selfie of the two of them.

"I heard there was an Egyptian obelisk somewhere in the park. It's supposed to be near the Metropolitan. Can we see that or is it too boring?"

"It's that way," Hunter said. "Near the Great Lawn and past Bethesda Terrace. We can see both and then start walking back. We should get reservations for dinner."

"I'll call the concierge at the hotel. They should be able to get us into one of the hotel restaurants or someplace nearby." Monty made the call as they made their way back to the dock. By the time they were out of the boat, Monty was done and they continued on their way. They saw the fountain in the terrace and the obelisk that Monty wanted to see, then wandered back through the park, past the hotel, and then on down Fifth Avenue.

Everywhere they looked, Monty saw something and bounced with excitement. He bounded up the steps of the New York Public Library and down the walk where the Rockefeller Center ice rink would be if it were cold enough. They got drinks, talked, laughed—it was an amazing day, and every second Hunter was hyperaware of each of Monty's smiles and every time he laughed. By the time they got back to the hotel, they were both tired. The concierge had done his best, but every spot in the hotel restaurants was booked, so Hunter ordered room service and changed into fresh clothes.

"I ordered some beer," Hunter called to Monty as a knock sounded on the door. He opened it to a chorus of greetings as a dozen men flooded into the room. So much for going out to a club. It looked like the party had come to them.

Hunter grinned and greeted each of the guys from the New York team. They were in different conferences, so they didn't play each other all that often. Some of them, he knew, were managed by Garvin and his organization. He had spoken to Billy last week and told him he'd be in town and where he was staying.

Of course their room service showed up shortly after that, but Hunter managed to salvage Monty's dinner and get it to him. It seemed he was content to stay in his room of the suite.

"You can come out and meet everyone," Hunter said.

"You have fun. I don't want to get in your way." He gave Hunter a half smile and thanked him for the dinner before closing the door. For some reason, Hunter felt that door closing was more ominous than just Monty not wanting to join the impending party.

"How long are you here?" Hershel, a huge defenseman, asked as he settled onto half the sofa. The man was built like a brick shithouse.

"Just a couple days. I have a meeting first thing in the morning, lunch, more meetings, and dinner. It's an all-day dog and pony show." He tried to downplay what was happening because the deal required secrecy. At least that's what Garvin always told him. Until any deal was done, keep your mouth shut. He hoped the guys would take the hint and not plan to stay half the night.

"Then let's head down to the bar and see what's happening," one of the guys suggested, and they all began to file out of the room. Hunter followed them, knowing Monty would be relieved. Besides, the guys tended to be a little physical, especially when they got a few drinks in them, so the bar was much safer than the hotel suite if there was damage done. Hunter had paid that huge bill before.

HUNTER RODE up in the elevator at nearly midnight. He'd had one hell of a time. Sure, he'd probably had one too many to drink, but he hadn't been driving, and it had been a blast to see the players. Hunter was quiet when he came in the suite and went to the bedroom, got undressed, climbed into bed, and fell to sleep in seconds.

CHAPTER 6

MONTY HAD drunk too much; he knew that. After Hunter had left, he'd been pissed, and since Hunter had left him all of the beer that he'd ordered when they'd placed the room service order, Monty drank every one. They had had a great day, just the two of them. He especially liked when Hunter tackled him on the lawn. Monty nearly went wild when Hunter's weight pressed against him. He might have felt some wood from Hunter, he wasn't sure, but it was pretty clear there was *something* between them.

And as Monty became aware of his surroundings and the beer haze dissipated, he realized he wasn't alone in bed. In fact, there was someone warm and very naked lying along his back and something hard pushed against his butt. All it took was a few seconds to get beyond the beer breath for him to smell Hunter's athletically intoxicating scent. Fucking hell, Hunter was in bed with him, naked, holding him, and Monty didn't dare move because it felt so amazingly good. A heated wall of muscle pressed to his back while arms of hot steel encircled him, making him feel safe. He closed his eyes and thanked his lucky stars for whatever brought Hunter to him. Instantly he was as hard as nails, pushing his ass back to rub along Hunter's impressive length.

Hunter groaned and pulled him closer, his hand sliding along his belly and then down to his hips. Monty shivered and bit his lower lip as Hunter gripped his cock, holding it tight and firm. This was a dream, it had to be a dream, but when Hunter stroked him slowly, Monty stretched, arching his back, pressing more firmly into Hunter.

"Damn, you feel good, baby," Hunter mumbled as he continued stroking.

70

"Hunter," Monty whimpered as Hunter rolled on top of him, pinning him to the mattress, and thrusted against him.

"Fuck, you shaved and feel so smooth. I like it." Hunter held him closer.

Monty realized that whatever dream Hunter was having, it wasn't about him. "Hunter," Monty said a little more forcefully and waited for him to snap out of whatever daze he was in. "*Hunter.*"

Hunter opened his eyes and smiled. "Monty." Hunter blinked. "What are you doing in my bed?"

"This is my bed. It seems you crawled in with me." He tried not to be mad, because who could be when waking up next to a god like that, but it did hurt that Hunter was getting frisky thinking about someone else. "You were having some sort of dream about a guy apparently, a hairy one."

"Oh God." Hunter rolled away and sat up. "I was asleep, and I had this dream that I was with an… old friend."

"Apparently this was an old friend whose dick you used to grab and one who was hairy, but you wished would shave or something. Not that I mind being awakened in a really nice way, but I do like it if the guy involved at least knows it's me in the room." Monty slid off the other side of the bed, grabbing the spread to wrap around him. "Maybe you should just go to your own room, and we'll forget this ever happened." Monty turned so he didn't see Hunter get out of the bed. "How much did you have to drink last night?"

"I don't know. Enough to come into the wrong bed, I guess." He opened the door and left the room. Once the door closed, Monty went into the bathroom.

What the hell had he just done? Hunter had been in his bed, and he just kicked him out.

"Because he thought you were someone else, dummy," Monty chastised his reflection in the mirror and then cleaned up and showered. He had to be ready for whatever Hunter needed him to do. And regardless of what had happened last night, he was still Hunter's assistant, at least for now, and he'd do his job. Once they got home, he could figure out what to do.

Monty dressed and got ready for the day. He left the room and was greeted with Hunter's closed bedroom door. "We need to leave in ten minutes."

"Okay," Hunter answered but didn't come out.

"Are you okay?" Maybe he'd really hurt Hunter.

"I don't know what to wear. Everything is…."

Monty opened the door and went inside. Hunter stood in a pair of briefs, holding up two pairs of pants with a half-dozen shirts on the bed. "You can pick anything. They'll all work." Monty paired a nice set of slacks and a shirt for him and tried not to look at the package on display right in front of him. Monty figured years of being in locker rooms had made Hunter less conscious of nudity or being scantily clad in front of others.

"Okay." Hunter pulled on his pants and then his shirt as Monty left the room. He closed the door behind him and waited for Hunter to finish.

"We need to go," Monty called, and Hunter came out, looking rattled and at loose ends. "This is a game day," Monty said, trying to make him feel better. "Put what happened out of your mind. It's fine, and you'd had too much to drink. It was a mistake, so just forget it. You didn't hurt me…." Just the opposite really.

"But I thought I—"

"You were sweet and sexy, but you thought I was someone else. That's all." Monty had let himself hope Hunter might have wanted to touch him that way, but he needed to get over it and move on. *Note to self, be sure to lock the door next time.* "Put it out of your mind, and if you want to talk about it later, we can. Right now, you have some important things you need to do."

"You sound like one of my coaches," Hunter told him.

"Okay, then. I'll take that as a compliment. I've already called for the car, and I have all the stuff I think we'll need, so let's go." He swatted Hunter's backside.

"What was that for?"

"Isn't that what coaches do to get you psyched up?" Monty was enjoying this way too much. "Yet another thing to love about sports.

Now let's go." He got Hunter moving, and they managed to make it to the lobby and out to the car without much fuss. They rode to breakfast, which was set up in a conference room of the office building where all the meetings were to take place. Hunter introduced him to Garvin, who shook his hand and promptly moved away to talk to people more important.

Monty basically took a seat in the corner, ate a bagel, and watched everyone mingle and get to know Hunter. He didn't blame them. Hunter was a celebrity, and he was the one they wanted to hire to sell whatever it was they sold. Monty got that.

Then it hit him—he wasn't jealous of Hunter as much as he was of Hunter's attention. He wanted to be the one talking and laughing with Hunter, like he'd been the day before. But that was stupid. He was only Hunter's assistant and nothing more. So they could have a good time together and they were both gay. That didn't mean they should have sex, fall in love, and live happily ever after. Hunter was important, and Monty was just the assistant. That was how it was, and there was nothing he could do about it. So Monty figured he may as well get used to it and move on. He was here to help Hunter and get whatever Hunter needed. That was his role, and he'd do his best for Hunter.

Monty set his bag aside and filled a cup with coffee just the way Hunter liked it. Then he took it to him, pressed it into his hand, and returned to his chair.

Monty listened to the conversation, and eventually everyone settled down for the meeting. They talked and reviewed everything, while Hunter nodded along. Because he'd told Hunter to wait for some zinger in the review, he listened as well, but none of this was his expertise. He was only Hunter's assistant, and his job was to get coffee, not negotiate contracts. They broke for lunch and had it delivered.

Hunter looked bored. The conversations now centered with Garvin, and Monty watched as Hunter disengaged and simply sat in his chair, slowly rolling it back and forth.

"Do we have a deal?" asked the man at the head of the table.

"Yes," Garvin agreed, and Hunter rose to shake hands with the men around the table.

"As you know, we have a very tight timetable. We need to get this endorsement up and running. Hunter's popularity and name recognition are good, but we want to make him a household name."

"Thank you, sir," Hunter said, as Monty scrambled to his feet, grabbing his bag, and then followed Hunter out of the room. "Garvin will take care of the rest of the deal." He seemed majorly relieved, and they left the office. "I want to go back to the hotel."

Monty called for the limousine, and the driver pulled around to meet them out front. Monty sat quietly across from Hunter, glancing at him and then looking anywhere else. He wanted to ask him if this was what Hunter really wanted to do, but it wasn't his place. They had been talking about billboards, signs, print ads, et cetera... in underwear. Granted, Monty had seen Hunter in nothing but underwear and he was stunning beyond belief, as far as Monty was concerned. But in private was one thing—sixty feet tall was quite another.

When they arrived at the hotel, Hunter climbed out of the car without saying anything and marched to the elevator. Monty got in with him but watched the display as they rose to their floor. Hunter didn't talk, and Monty stayed silent too. The tension in the small space mounted by the second. Monty wasn't really sure why, at least not completely. But once the doors slid open, Hunter strode to the room and, once inside, went right to his bedroom and closed the door forcefully.

Monty went to his room, shut the door silently, and pulled out his phone.

"How's New York?" Collin asked as soon as he answered the phone. Collin had come out of the closet as a junior, and he and Monty had been best friends. They'd been two gay boys against the world, and it had pretty much worked for them. Of course, because Collin was now in Chicago, their friendship consisted of Skype calls and e-mails, but they were still close.

"I got a new job working as a personal assistant for a football player."

"Oh God, douse my nuts in honey and stick me on a fire-ant hill." Collin was always very dramatic. It worked for him, as he was a scene artist and creator for the Lyric Opera. "That must be hell."

"He's the gay one," Monty said softly, "and he's…."

"A dreamboat?" Collin asked.

"Hot as all hell. But I don't understand him. I'm his assistant, but I see him watching me, and Lord knows… I like him. He's a good guy, and sometimes I think he likes me, but then he backs away, and then I back away because he backs away."

"So you want to ride his hobby horse?"

"He hasn't even kissed me yet, so we aren't up to hobby horses. But he was in bed with me. He was drunk and climbed into my bed instead of his, and I woke up this morning to big arms around me, a big chest pressed to my back, and a bigger… well, you get the picture. So I think he's interested. Hunter put the moves on me in his sleep, and he thought I was some other guy, and it creeped me out. But until then I liked it…."

"Did you ask him about it?"

"I tried, but Hunter got weird, and I felt weird, so he left, and I acted like some blushing virgin who'd just given her goodies to the evil knight. I keep thinking I should just be his assistant and let the rest go. He was drunk, and he ended up in my bed by mistake, and he was dreaming, and that's all there is to it."

"That sounds like you have all the answers you need. It was only a dream. Let it go and move on."

"Yeah…."

"Except…," Collin said. "I know there must be more than just that or you wouldn't be calling me with your princess panties all in a bunch. My guess is that something about this guy had gotten under your skin, and you don't know what to do about it."

"I guess."

"And if you think I have answers for you, I don't. My own love life is a complete and total mess. My latest boyfriend turned out to be a lying sack of shit."

"Was he cheating on you?"

"No. He tried to get me to go into business with him, and then I found out it was a real scam and he was in on it. What a disaster." Monty could see Collin's hands going in every direction. He always had a great flair.

"Sorry."

"Not a big deal now I know what's going on."

"So what do I do?" Monty asked.

"Have you talked to him about it? You work for the guy, and he's probably as turned around as you are. Clear the air and get on with it. That's all you can do."

"What if he fires me?" Monty's foot bounced on the floor.

"Then collect unemployment and move on, I guess. Look, he's your boss and all that. Just be professional and let what happened be a mistake and move on if you can. If not, get another job. Honey, I have to go. I have a tenor and a soprano who are about to come to blows, and I need to figure out what's going on before the entire opera world comes crashing down around us." Collin hung up, and Monty put his phone aside. He'd hoped Collin would have some different advice, but other than being someone to talk to, he'd said what Monty already thought.

Monty left the room. Hunter's door was still closed. He knocked softly and heard Hunter grunt something, so he cracked it open slightly.

"Hunter?" he asked, swinging it a little wider. "Are you all right?"

"Yes. Just tired and still hungover a little."

Monty got a glass of bottled water and brought it to Hunter.

"You need to drink. It'll help."

Hunter sat up and drank the water. "I'm sorry for last night. I honestly thought I was in my own room and...."

Monty nodded. "Okay."

"You don't believe me?" Hunter asked. "You think I came into your room to assault you or—"

"Whoa. Time out." Monty made a T with his hands. Where did that come from? Maybe this football stuff was rubbing off on him. "You got into bed with me because you thought it was your bed and you'd had too much to drink, right?" Hunter nodded. "There was no assaulting. As near as I can tell, there was some holding and some touching, both were quite nice, but there wasn't any assaulting."

"Then why were you so upset if you liked it?" Hunter asked.

"Because you thought you were doing that to someone else. You were dreaming and talking in your sleep, and I thought you were talking to me at first, but you obviously weren't." He held up his hands. "It's okay. There's no need to get upset or crazy. You didn't hurt me or do anything to me other than turn my crank a little." That's what he got for talking to Collin. "It's all right."

"But… then why are you so quiet?"

"Because you've been quiet, and I'm your assistant, remember? I'm supposed to make sure you're happy and try to give you your space if you need it, and I thought that was what you wanted. I know this has got you upset, and I'm sorry for that. So let's forget it happened and move on." God, why in the hell was that so hard to say? He didn't want to move on—he wanted to go back to being in bed with Hunter, only this time Hunter would know it was him. "So we have dinner tonight, and then, as far as I know, there is a photo shoot tomorrow. I should call Helen and see if she knows anything." Monty stood up to go, but Hunter stopped him.

"You have to know I'd never hurt you."

"I know that, Hunter. It was a mistake, and we can leave it at that."

Surprising how much those words hurt to say.

DINNER THAT evening was a grand affair. Monty was shocked that Hunter wanted him there, but he went along. Except for Hunter trying to include him in the conversation, Monty was ignored by everyone.

He was an assistant, a servant, someone to look around and over in favor of the star of the evening.

"You hate this, don't you?" Hunter asked once they were done eating and yet another round of drinks was brought for everyone.

"It doesn't matter what I think, Hunter. I'm here for you. Do you need anything?" He stared at the drink that had been placed in front of Hunter. He knew Hunter didn't like whiskey. "I can get you a beer if you like."

"These aren't beer people," Hunter whispered as laughter went up from the table. Hunter's nerves were evident, the energy rolling off him. "Sometimes I think I'm just some pawn to these guys."

"Maybe, but remember why you're doing this. Football will only last so long. So make the money you can so you can live the rest of your life." Monty winked conspiratorially and went to try to find something else for Hunter to drink. He left the private room of the restaurant they were in, with its glitter of gold and deep wood accents. The place looked more like a palace than a restaurant, and the prices would bankrupt royalty.

"I'd like a beer for Mr. Davis, please," he told the server who had been helping them.

"Of course. I'll bring it right in." He hurried away, and Monty went to the restroom.

"Did you hear that hick football player George hired?" one guy at the urinal was saying with his back to him. Monty opened one of the stall doors, went inside, and closed it.

"All that matters is that he's the sports pick of the week. They'll use his pictures, sell a ton of stuff, and then dump him as soon as the whole thing blows over. I mean, really. The guy is good-looking, but do they really think guys are going to run out and buy stuff from a man like him?" A flush followed, and then the door opened and banged closed.

Monty took care of business before washing his hands and leaving the restroom. He was so angry, he wanted to spit. He hadn't recognized the voice right off, but as soon as he returned to the table, he paid close attention to who said what.

"This is going to be a great campaign," a voice Monty now recognized clearly said from one chair down. The voice's owner stood and offered a glass to the man at the head of the table.

Two-faced asshole.

Monty raised his glass as the others did and tried his best not to glare at the man. Monty did catch Garvin's eye for a second and wondered how he could tell him what he'd heard, but Garvin went back to his conversation.

The meal seemed to go on forever before ending with a chocolate-mint dessert, and finally everyone got up to leave. Most of the people at the table were nearly drunk. Monty had soda for most of the evening, not wanting a repeat of the night before, and he noticed that Hunter had nursed his whiskey for at least an hour. Monty was never so happy to climb into the back of the limousine.

"Those people are assholes," he said as soon as the door closed. "The guy who gave the toast is a pile of shit, and I wanted to smack him."

"Why?"

"He called you names in the bathroom, the asshat." Monty clenched his fists. "He said you were the flavor of the month or something like that."

"I know. I'm a successful gay football player. There are people who want me to succeed, those who want me to fail, and everyone wants to make money off me, one way or another. I'm playing well, and I'm a novelty. I know that, and so does Garvin."

"And you're happy with that?"

"I'm…." He sighed. "Like you said, I'm going to make what I can while I can, so I can have a good life for years. I know what some people think about me, and I care but I don't care. My life as a football player has a shelf life. The average career in the league is only two or three years. It's a punishing job, and most guys get injured or just can't cut it." Hunter shifted seats to sit next to him. "But I appreciate your getting angry on my behalf."

"How can you just take that?" Monty felt his anger rising again. "You're a good person, and you're so much better than this."

"Because I have to. I don't have any other choice." Hunter's voice was so calm. "I play football, and I know the rules, so I can play by them and win games. When it comes to these endorsements, Garvin knows the same thing, and he doesn't make money unless I make money. Hopefully I'll have a long career, but as a hedge in case I don't, I have to do things like have pictures taken in my underwear."

Hunter touched his chin, and Monty turned toward him. "Is it in the assistant's handbook for you to care what happens to me?"

"No. I think that's in my own handbook. I don't want them taking advantage of you." Monty blinked as Hunter got closer. "What are you doing?" Monty asked.

Hunter's answer was to kiss him.

At first all Monty could wonder was if this was a good idea, but Hunter's lips tugged at his and he let it go. He wanted to be kissed, and damn if Hunter wasn't mind-blowing, and he tasted even better with the hint of chocolate mint on his lips. Hunter tugged him closer and wrapped his strong arms around him the way they'd been that morning when he'd woken up. This was probably one hell of a mistake, but Monty didn't care at that moment. The car hit some rough road, Monty bounced slightly, and Hunter ended up on top of him, pressing him into the seat. Hunter kissed him deeper, holding tighter as the leather pressed to his back, the scent of Hunter filling his nostrils.

"Hunter, are you sure about this?"

"I know who I'm kissing if that's what you're asking. There's no doubt about that," he whispered, then returned his lips to Monty's.

God, this is what Monty wanted, and he slid his hands under Hunter's shirt and up his back, stroking the powerful muscles he found there. Hunter's strength was a turn-on. Monty was well aware Hunter could manhandle him to wherever he wanted, but he was gentle and the way he held him communicated care and firmness rather than domination.

The car lurched a final time and then slowly came to a stop. Hunter backed away and Monty sat up, straightened his clothes, and gathered his bag. There was no way in hell he was going to walk through the Plaza hotel looking like he'd just been kissed within an inch of his life, even if it was true.

Monty climbed out after Hunter, and they hurried to the elevator while trying not to look like they were in a rush.

"Hunter," Garvin said, crossing the lobby toward them.

Monty groaned at the interruption. They all headed to the elevator. He would have liked more time alone with Hunter. Garvin and Hunter talked business, and Monty tried to look as though he were giving them their privacy, but what he really wanted was for Garvin to disappear in a puff of smoke or something. He hoped Garvin would go to his own room, but instead he followed Hunter to his and settled on the sofa.

"I'm going to order a snack," Garvin said, reaching for the phone. "We need to celebrate this deal. It's signed, and the initial payment is on its way. Today was one hell of a payday."

"Yeah, and now my work begins. I have an appointment first thing in the morning, and you know how these things go. They take a lot of time and energy." Hunter glanced toward the door, but Garvin wasn't getting the message. "And it's getting late."

"I see," Garvin said, finally understanding. He stood and turned to Monty with a gaze as cold as ice. Monty turned away and went to his room to get away from the look that froze his blood. "Hunter, is there something I need to know?"

"No," Hunter answered flatly. Monty could hear what they were saying through the cracked door. "I think it's time for this day to end. I have to be up early and looking good. You need to be up too, because you're going to be there as well."

"I'm not needed...."

"I don't care. You need to go back to your room, get some sleep, because you will be there to watch the photo session. Because I said so." Hunter was angry, and Monty put his hand over his mouth, wishing he could see the look on Garvin's face. He'd never met him before today, and what he had seen, Monty didn't particularly like. "I need some rest, and I think you need to sober up from all you drank at

81

dinner. I didn't know you were a lush, so maybe when you're thinking clearer, we can talk about what's coming next."

"You... you...."

The tone was all Monty needed to hear.

"Hunter, I have your schedule for tomorrow, and we need to go over it," Monty said as he strode back into the living room, to remind both of them he was still there and to try to cool the emotions in the room before either of them said something they'd regret. Hell, he half expected them to challenge each other to rulers at midnight to measure their dicks. "We have to be at the photographer's at eight, so we'll need to be up at six thirty and ready to go by seven fifteen." He turned to Garvin. "Are you going to meet us there?"

"I'll ride with you in the limousine."

Way to suck all the fun out of it. "Fine. Then we'll see you at seven fifteen in the lobby. The session will most likely take all morning, and then tomorrow afternoon we'll head back to Philadelphia. I have your schedule for the rest of the week, but we can review that on the way home." He hoped like hell that Garvin wasn't going with them.

"Once the shoot is over, I want to do some shopping before we leave town. So we'll stop by Bergdorf's on our way. I'm trying to update my image," Hunter added to Garvin.

"I need to leave in the late morning."

"Then you can make sure everything is all set at the shoot and that there are no issues before you go." Hunter patted Garvin on the shoulder with what seemed like more force than was necessary. "Have a good night, and I'll see you in the lobby in the morning." Hunter walked to the door and opened it, letting Garvin out. Once the door was shut, Hunter said, "God, whenever he drinks, he turns into the biggest dick I know."

"I was beginning to wonder."

"He's a great agent, but the man can't hold his booze. Garvin will be fine once he sleeps it off." Hunter swallowed hard, and Monty felt his gaze rake over him like a heat ray. Monty wanted to continue what they'd started in the car, but maybe that wasn't such a good idea.

"I think we need to say good night," Monty said as Hunter took a step forward. "You're my boss, and before things get too out of hand and we do things that we can't step back from, we should leave it at that."

"Fine," Hunter said, but continued coming closer. Monty knew he should stop him, but Hunter pulled him right against his hotness, tilted his head upward, and kissed him hard.

Monty's entire body thrummed, and he knew he was a goner. He wanted Hunter so damn bad he couldn't move or think. He moaned softly and was about to take a step back toward his room to invite Hunter inside with him when Hunter pulled back, breaking the kiss, leaving him gasping.

"Good night, Monty." Hunter crossed the living area and closed the door to his room behind him.

Monty was completely stunned beyond belief as he went into his own room. How in the hell was he supposed to go to sleep after that?

CHAPTER 7

HUNTER DRESSED, choosing whatever he wanted from the color-sorted closet. When he stepped out, Monty was waiting for him. "Do I look all right?"

"You do. I had some breakfast sent up for you. We don't have much time." Monty motioned to the table. "Go ahead and eat while I get us packed. I figure we can leave right from the shoot." Monty went into Hunter's room and, five minutes later, emerged with his suitcase, which he set next to the door where his own bag rested already. Then he went through the suite before joining him.

"Aren't you having some?" Hunter pointed to the breakfast tray.

"No. I already ate." He sounded so cold.

"What's going on?"

"What do you want from me?" Monty asked and handed him a newsstand rag. "It says here that I'm your boy toy and they have a picture of the two of us in Central Park. I didn't even think of anyone watching, but someone sure as hell was. Look at this, there's a picture of when you tackled me. Of course it's all innuendo...."

"I didn't know."

"I'm not saying you did. But you kissed me on the way home last night and then in the room before we went to bed. So is kissing you and waking up with you part of my job description? They sure as hell make it sound like it is."

Hunter grabbed the newspaper and stared at the pictures. "That's just a rag that will print anything they like. We were having fun in the park yesterday, and someone took pictures." Hunter threw the paper to the floor. "And no, kissing me or anything else is not part of your job description." Hunter felt his chest tighten, and he took deep breaths. "This is all bullshit and lies."

Monty turned away. "We need to go now or you'll be late."

"So this is how you want to handle things? Pulling away and acting cold?" Hunter was trying to understand. He'd been warned scandals like this could happen, and he could take it if they were only attacking him, but they were going after the people near him and that was below the belt as far as he was concerned.

"I don't have much choice. In their view I'm some whore who's after your money and hitching onto you for something."

"It doesn't matter what they said. We were only playing football and having some fun," Hunter explained. "We didn't do anything wrong." He bent down and picked up the paper. "This thing is only good for lining cages and letting birds and hamsters poop on it."

"But what are the people we met yesterday going to think when they see this? They're going to freak." Monty stood straighter. "So I need to appear as the perfect assistant, and you have to stop looking at me. I see you sometimes, and other people will too."

"So what do you want?"

"I don't know. I thought I might last night, but this… this could hurt your career and your chances at more endorsements." Monty was becoming frantic.

"No, it won't. If anything, this is going to make people wonder about the kind of person I am. Everyone knows these stories are fake. They take a few pictures, create a wild story, and then try to let the pictures be the proof, but it doesn't work. It's obvious in the picture that we were playing football. We have jerseys on, and there's the ball right there. This is stupid. So don't get upset."

"What about Garvin?"

"Please. Football players have been indicted for drugs and dog fighting, beating up spouses, and God knows what else. Nobody is going to get in a twist over football players playing football." He tossed the paper in the trash. "Why don't we get going?"

Monty nodded and joined him at the door. "If you say so. You're the one with something to lose… well, a lot more than me."

Hunter stopped shy of opening the door. "Reputations are important, and there's nothing that says your reputation is worth less

85

than mine." He opened the door and grabbed his bag. At the elevator they were met by a bellhop who escorted them down. Hunter took care of the bill, and they met Garvin in the lobby. He looked like he'd worked himself up.

"Did you see it?"

"Yeah. Personally I thought the pictures of us playing football in the park were pretty good." Hunter was determined to downplay this and continued through the lobby to the car. He left the luggage with the driver and climbed in the back, followed by Garvin and Monty. "It's nothing. Some people took our picture, and a fiction writer got ahold of it."

"People will talk," Garvin said.

"So? You always said the one thing we should always worry about is when no one is talking about me. So let it go." Hunter refrained from looking at Monty as they pulled away from the curb. He was already getting tired of this whole situation.

AT THE studio, the photographer was setting up, and Hunter was whisked away to makeup and to get ready, with Monty following along. As Hunter sat in the chair, the shoot director, Sebastian, sat in the chair next to him.

"We have three different looks for you. We'll go through each one and see how they work. The biggest thing is to relax and let it happen."

"I'm fine in front of the camera. I work with cameras all around me. I know this is different, but I'm not intimidated." After all, he was photographed naked a week ago. At least today he'd have something on.

"Monty, do they have coffee?"

"I'll get you some," Monty said as he hurried away.

"Can I ask you a question? Is he seeing anyone?" Sebastian asked. "I know this is unusual, but he's adorable, and I was wondering if I had a shot with him."

Hunter stilled, not sure how he should answer him. It wasn't as though he had a claim on Monty, but the thought of telling this guy that he was free left him with a sour taste in his mouth.

"I'm not sure how to answer you," Hunter finally said. "He lives in Philadelphia and…."

"I understand," Sebastian said and moved away as the makeup artist got into position. "Nothing too heavy. We want him to look natural. So bring out his eyes just a little and make his lips pop. The rest he'll be able to do on his own."

"What do you understand?" Hunter asked before Sebastian could leave.

Monty arrived with his coffee, handed it to him, and stood nearby while he finished up.

Sebastian shook his head. "I'll be out there when you're ready." He left, and Hunter followed him with his eyes before glancing at Monty, who had apparently noticed Hunter watching Sebastian and looked about ready to spit jealous nails.

"Thank you, Monty." He smiled at him as the artist finished up.

"Go ahead and wow them," she said and stepped away. "You are going to rock this thing, I know it."

"Thank you." He set the coffee aside, realizing he was going to alter the makeup if he drank. He headed out with Monty following.

"Sebastian asked me if you were seeing anyone," Hunter told him quietly while the photographer finished setting up.

"What did you tell him?"

Hunter shrugged. "I didn't know what to say, but he was interested in you and I got jealous, so I tried to discourage him." Monty stopped walking for a moment.

"We're almost ready for you," the photographer called.

Hunter went behind a screen, got into a pair of low-rise white briefs, and stepped out onto the set.

The photographer came over immediately. "Sorry for not introducing myself earlier. I'm Jonah Myers, and this is going to be great. We'll take our time and get some amazing images." He shook

Hunter's hand and turned back to his team. "We're doing this in color. So many of these ads are black and white, but with his skin tone, these pictures are going to pop like mad." Jonah got into position and began shooting frame after frame. "You're strong and fully dressed in a power suit. Nothing can touch you."

Hunter imagined what he asked and stood taller, head facing just off to the side, toward Monty.

"That's incredible. Keep that up. Look to the other side." Hunter did, his gaze falling onto a blank wall. The photographer put down his camera. "I need you to keep that expression."

"What expression?"

"The smoldering heat. For just a few seconds, you stood tall and broad and looked like you were about to burst into flame with desire. It filled your eyes. I need that. We aren't going to bring in someone else—the image is just you—but we need to feel as though the real subject of the image isn't here." He set the camera on a stool and walked over to him. "This is all about illusion. We're selling underwear, for God's sake. Something everyone wears every day, and yet we want it to seem glamorous and exotic."

"Okay. I get that, but…." Hunter wasn't a model. He was just an athlete they'd brought in because he had the look the company wanted. But he was going to do his best. Hunter just needed a little more direction from the photographer.

"Yes. You're in your underwear, and you're hot and powerful, and every guy wants to be you. But most guys' underwear is bought by the women in their lives. So when they see this image, we want them to think that they can place themselves in it. That if they buy this underwear, their husbands will look like you in it. Because let's face it, who wouldn't want to come home to this every day instead of a balding middle-aged guy with a beer gut. So let's try to give them that."

"Okay. I will," Hunter said. He wasn't quite sure how he was going to achieve that.

"Just take your time and relax. Sometimes it takes a few minutes to warm up in front of the camera." He returned to fetch his camera off the stool. "That's it, again, you're powerful. Nothing can touch you. I need heat and fire."

Hunter thought of the crunch of battle when he was on the field, the tension, the pressure, and the way everything fired all at once. It was a rush, and his muscles filled with blood as his heart raced faster.

"You're a warrior," Jonah said. "I see that, but what are you fighting for? That's it, move through the space. Try different angles." He continued to click frame after frame as Hunter shifted from side to side and even crouched a little, and then Jonah put down the camera with a sigh. "We got some amazing images. Why don't you switch to the boxer briefs?" There was clearly something he was looking for and not getting. Hunter wished he knew what that was and how to make it happen. He went behind the screen, changed, and adjusted his junk in the mirror.

He'd been afraid that, with all the excitement, he'd get excited, but there was no chance of that happening. This was hard work, and it wasn't particularly glamorous at all.

Hunter stepped back onto the set, and one of the assistants adjusted the garment while he stood still.

"I don't like those on you," Jonah said.

Hunter looked down at himself. "Okay…." He felt Monty's eyes on him and knew he was watching even though Hunter couldn't see him.

Jonah chuckled. "Not that you look bad in them, it's that they don't convey…. You're all about banked power that's ready to strike, feral, raw muscle. These are more for a guy from the boardroom who doesn't want ass lines under his clothes."

Hunter smiled at the joke, and Jonah hurried to his camera and snapped picture after picture.

"That was awesome." He motioned Hunter over, and he looked at the pictures on the monitor. "Those are perfect for this. That smile and the way you're holding your hands. You're not taking yourself too seriously in these, and it comes through beautifully. Go ahead and change. We're done with those."

89

When he got back behind the curtain, he found a black pair of wide-banded, tiny bikini briefs. They didn't look big enough to cover much of anything, and when he put them on, they barely covered his pubes and he was sure his buttcrack was showing to a degree. He didn't want to step out—he felt so exposed—but he did.

No one seemed to notice. They were all going about their work. He stepped in front of the white background and stood in the center.

"You look like you want to run away and hide," Jonah told him. "Remember you're strong and nothing can touch you, just like at the beginning. And I need that heat, even more than the first time. You need to smolder. I have the power, but not the heat. I know you can do this, Hunter," Jonah said as he continued snapping image after image.

Hunter tried imagining various things. Someone moved outside the camera range, but it was hard for him to see past the lights. Then Monty stepped into view, staring at him, mouth open, his eyes filled with naked want. Hunter's heartbeat quickened, his pulse raced, and he grew warm.

"Holy mother of God," Jonah said as he continued snapping pictures. Hunter was only mildly aware of him. For a few seconds, everything slipped away except Monty. "Turn slightly. Yes, that's perfect." Flash after flash continued as Hunter moved and changed positions, but this time Monty stayed in his line of sight. Wherever he looked, Monty was there, moving in the background, and Hunter wanted him.

"Okay, that's a wrap," Jonah said. Hunter was breathing hard like he'd just run the race of his life. "You were amazing, and I have to tell you that when you got it, you got it. Look at these images."

Monty handed him a robe. "You better put this on before everyone gets a gander at things you don't want them to see," he said in his ear. Hunter shrugged into the soft white robe and joined Jonah at the monitor. Image after image shone on the screen, and Hunter was taken aback. Even he could see the power and felt the heat. It was awesome.

"You did amazing. I've known professional models who were unable to do what you just did. You figured it out, turned it on, and these images are going to be everywhere. The first ones are good, but these are wonderful. Go on and get dressed. You did great today." He clapped Hunter on the shoulder and then turned back to the monitor.

"Where's Garvin?" Hunter asked Monty.

"He left just before you started shooting. I think he was bored because there really was nothing for him to do. Garvin did say he'd call you tomorrow." Monty looked relieved. "He was kind of gruff, but he was nicer than he was last night."

"I'm going to change, and we can get out of here."

"Did you really want to go shopping, or was that a ploy to get Garvin out of your hair?" Monty asked.

Hunter stepped behind the screen and changed into his regular clothes. "Let's go shopping. I'd like some really dressy shirts and things." He peered around the screen, hoping Monty understood that they were in public and he wanted to answer the question without saying something potentially gossipworthy. "We don't have to go nuts, but maybe we can find some things that will look nice on me where I can actually see the color."

"All right, then."

"I'm almost done here, so get your things and call the driver so we can go." Hunter finished dressing and then thanked the photographer and everyone else. He and Monty were about to leave when Jonah hurried up to them, catching them at the door.

"I wanted you to know that I'd work with you anytime. You're a great model, and if you're willing, I can get you all the work you want." He handed Hunter his business card, and Monty started to fish around in his bag.

"Just call Monty. He's the keeper of my schedule, and he can help you with anything you need." Hunter grinned, and Monty fished again and came up with a piece of paper, which he wrote his number on and handed to Jonah. "I'd be happy to work with you again."

They shook hands, and then he and Monty left the studio.

"I was about to give him Garvin's card."

"He's a sports agent, and this is my own deal. I want some control over my life. I'm sure you can handle anything that needs to be done." They reached the sidewalk and climbed into the limousine.

"So I take it you think I'm no longer on probation?" Monty asked.

"I was an idiot. You are a great assistant." Hunter sat next to Monty. "You saved me in there. I wasn't sure what the hell he wanted me to do, and then you were there, and bam, it happened just like that." Hunter put an arm around Monty's shoulders and lightly traced his thumb across his lips.

"I hope you know we are not doing anything in the back of a car," Monty said with a slight scowl.

"You aren't interested in making out in the back of a limo?" Hunter did his best to seem aghast and then broke into a grin. "I have no intention of doing anything here. You deserve something better and much more comfortable." Hunter angled closer, heat flaring between them, but the car pulled to a stop and the driver opened the door, interrupting the moment. For some damn reason, that always seemed to happen.

THE RIDE home seemed to go on forever. They stopped at Bergdorf's along the way, and Hunter got an amazing silk shirt that felt as light and slick on his skin as he hoped Monty would when he was finally able to get him home… alone. He found a color that looked okay to him, and Monty said it would go beautifully with his other things. Hunter had Monty pick one out for himself for all his help, and Hunter got a few other things as well. The purchases were in the trunk along with their bags. Hunter sat on one of the seats with Monty across from him with his computer on his lap.

"I've asked you before, but don't you ever stop?"

"I guess not." Monty's phone rang, and he and Helen talked for a while. "Okay. I'll make those additions and changes." He hung up and continued working. "Sometimes I swear trying to keep up with your schedule is nearly as difficult as it would be for the president. The dang thing seems to change by the hour. Garvin set you up with a meeting next week to put your face on a cereal box or something. Maybe they want you to do commercials for the cereal. It's at his office, and I have it on the schedule. She said Garvin is still fuming about the article, but your publicist is apparently having a field day with it, talking about your love of the game and playing in Central Park."

"I told you everything would be okay."

"Yeah, but while we were playing football, it was more than that when they snapped that picture."

"Yeah, I know. But no one needs to know that until we want to talk about it." Hunter sat back, watching Monty as he worked.

"One more thing," Monty said. "I know you're being nice and all, but you don't need to be buying me things. The jersey was nice, and I like the shirt, I really do, but it was too much. You shouldn't spend your money on me like that."

"But you looked nice in it, and—"

"That isn't the point. I don't want to be bought and paid for. Just treat me well. I know you were being nice, but being good to me is more important than buying me stuff." Monty turned his attention back to his computer, and Hunter tried to make sense of what he'd just said.

"That's the same thing." He was getting confused. Hunter knew he wasn't the smartest bulb on the string. Lord, that had been made perfectly clear to him his entire life. *"Play football and play hard so you'll make it big. It's your only chance."* His father's words from when Hunter was twelve still rang in his ears too damn often.

"No, it isn't. Being nice to people is taking them out to dinner, saying pleasant things. It's easy and superficial. Like today when you were having trouble in the photo shoot. You looked great on the outside, but there was nothing underneath. But when you let some of who you are on the inside come through, it made for stunning images, and that's being good to someone. That comes from inside, and it's so much more than being nice." Monty set his computer aside. "I know I confuse you sometimes, but I don't want just the Hunter who's gorgeous and stunning, with eyes as blue as the deepest ocean and with pecs and a stomach that could be used as a cheese grater. Granted, those are hot, but they're on the surface. It's the man underneath who's really important. He's the professional football player who took me to Central Park to toss the football so I could learn a little more about his world. He's the one who rented me a boat because he saw how excited I was. It couldn't have been much fun for you to watch me play with it for half an hour."

"Actually, it was the highlight of the day," Hunter said softly.

"See. That's being good to someone. You did something to make me happy. My mom used to say it wasn't the stuff she bought us that we'd remember, but the stuff we did and the time we spent, which was strange because those were the things she didn't do, but I guess she thought she did. I stopped trying to figure her out a long time ago."

"I think I understand." He wasn't sure how happy he was and wondered if he should take the shirt back but kept quiet. He'd given it to Monty, and he wanted him to have it. "But look at it this way. You made me feel good in clothes, and I never did before, so I want you to feel the same way."

"Okay. I can live with that." Monty bounded across the limo to sit next to him. "Just don't think you need to do it again. Okay? You pay me to be your assistant, and it's hard enough understanding where being your assistant ends and whatever this is—" He slipped his hand under Hunter's shirt, and Hunter closed his eyes, relishing the gentle, caring touch. "—begins."

"Monty—"

"You have to try to look at this from my side, okay? I like you. I think you're an amazing guy, but I need a job and working for you is pretty awesome. But I don't want to think that sleeping with you is part of the job, and I don't want anyone else to think that either. That tabloid article insinuated just that. Did you read what they said?"

Hunter shrugged.

"Why not?"

"Because...." Hunter slid away. "Because I don't...." He huffed. "Why do you think I have you review my schedule with me and never look at what you print out? I ask you questions all the time because I can't read very well. I played football, so no one gave a crap about whether I could read or write. Half the time I sat in the back of the class, doodling in notebooks and trying not to fall asleep as the material went further and further over my head. No one cared."

"So what did you do before I got here?"

"I tried to remember everything, and then I'd be late and sometimes forget about things. Helen used to call and remind me, and I'd do better when she did that. But there was too much, and everything got jumbled in my head, so I was always behind, but I didn't want anyone to know I couldn't read very well. I'm twenty-three years old and my two older sisters both have children. One is four years old, and the last time I visited, he came up to me carrying a book and I nearly panicked because I was afraid he'd want me to read it to him."

"Do they know?"

Hunter shook his head. "No one does, and they didn't care enough to find out. My dad only wanted me to play football, and my mom went along with what he said. I was the boy, so I was in my father's domain. So as long as I could catch a pass and run like the wind, that was all he gave a fuck about."

Monty moved closer and hugged him. "Do you want to do something about it?"

"What can I do? The last thing I need is the world knowing I can't read for shit. Not that it's particularly surprising for guys like me. But still...."

"I didn't ask that. I wondered if you wanted some help with your reading skills. If you wanted to change that—because you can if that's what you want."

"How?" Hunter had spent so many years at the bottom of the well of lies he'd created around his inability to read, he didn't think there was a way out of it.

Monty backed away, staring into his eyes. "Is that what you want?" he asked firmly.

"Yes. Of course I do."

"Then leave it to me."

"Are you going to teach me?" Hunter asked, feeling relieved that the circle of people aware of his deficiency remained as small as possible. He really thought he was missing something. Learning had always been hard for him. Being physical was easy—his muscles adapted quickly to just about anything—but getting anything to sink into his head was hard. Well, anything other than football. That came easily. Reading, math, science, English, all those things were just foreign to him. In school he'd liked some subjects, and of course he'd excelled in PE as well as woodshop and metal-working classes. They'd allowed him to work with his hands.

"No, I'm not really qualified to help you, and my dyslexia would get in the way, but I know someone who is, and they'll keep quiet if I tell them to." Monty smirked. "At least she will unless she wants me to tell her girlfriend every embarrassing story I know about my sister from high school. That girl was a menace to everyone."

Fear welled from deep inside Hunter. He could face down a defensive line without blinking for a second, but the thought of learning to read left him cold. Failure was not an option—his father had always made that clear enough, and he'd already failed to learn how to read and write well. He didn't need to repeat that. "I'm not sure about this...."

"What do you have to lose?"

"But what if I can't learn?"

"Of course you can. You're a smart man."

"No, I'm not. I know that. I never have been." He turned to look out the window. This whole conversation was hitting way too close to the tender spot at the core of him. He was a football player—that was it and all he was ever going to be. He had accepted that a long time ago, and when he made the pros, he determined he was going to make every cent he could while he had the chance so he wouldn't have to take some shit job when it was over. "All I am is the guy who catches passes for the Red Hawks. I'm fast and have magic hands. The rest of me...."

"Can be whatever you want. But you didn't get to be good at football or anything physical unless you practiced, and it's the same thing here. We all learn different things with practice."

"You make it sound so simple."

"And you make improving your reading skills sound as daunting as climbing Mount Everest. It doesn't have to be that way." Monty moved back to the other seat. "Just think about it. I don't mean to push you into something you don't want. I was only trying to help."

Hunter sighed and continued looking out the window. "I've spent so much of my life trying to cover up for the fact that I wasn't a good reader that I became good at covering up. I don't have to read anything ever. I don't get a newspaper, and there aren't even any books in the house. I watch television to find out what's going on, or someone else reads things to me. It's like the color-blindness thing. I've hidden it for so long that I've gotten used to it."

"You know you're not alone. I'm dyslexic. I see things differently when I read. I had to learn to deal with it. But up until then, people called me a dummy. I think I told you that. And I was lucky enough that someone saw it and helped me."

"No one stepped in to help me." The car grew quiet for a while. As he replayed the conversation, Hunter realized that he'd sounded whiny and a little childish. If he could stare down linebackers and tackles to make plays, he could certainly handle someone teaching him something as basic as how to read better.

"Maybe you never recognized when someone was trying to help."

Hunter had no argument to that.

MONTY'S WORDS hovered over him for the rest of the trip. Had he been turning away the help he needed because he hadn't wanted to recognize it? Or was he just scared? Hunter hated fear, or at least uncontrolled fear. On the gridiron, fear could make you sharp and help make plays happen, as long as it was controlled. If you let it run your life, it was debilitating, and on the field, that was when you did something stupid that got you or someone else hurt.

"Sir, we'll be at your destination in about ten minutes," the driver said over the intercom, and Hunter thanked him.

"What do I have tomorrow?" Hunter asked. "God, I hope it isn't too much."

"The day is free as far as I know. On Thursday there's another team meeting. It's apparently to go over the training-camp schedule and arrangements. Things like that. Of course Thursday is also your dad's old-guy party day."

"Shit...," he swore under his breath. He needed to put an end to that kind of stuff. His dad and his friends could watch the games at one of their houses. He'd been putting off the conversation, but he needed to have it sooner rather than later.

"I have a call tomorrow with a maid service to come in once a week and clean for you." Monty went through his notes. "I think that's it for the week unless Garvin has something that Helen hasn't told me about yet. This weekend there's a party at Joe's. He sent an e-mail invitation, and I responded for you."

"How did you do that?"

"Helen added me to the account. She set it up for you, remember? You never check it, so I do and saw the invitation." Monty set his phone on top of the laptop. "You can rest tomorrow and hopefully catch up from the past few days."

"Come here," Hunter said, and when Monty returned to the seat next to him, Hunter hugged him. "You really do care, don't you?"

"Of course I do. Why wouldn't I?" Monty lifted his gaze until he looked into Hunter's eyes. "Maybe the question is why would you think someone wouldn't care?"

For a few seconds, Hunter was stripped emotionally naked, or at least he felt as though he were. He did have his secrets, and Monty's question was dangerously close to the one he held tightest and never talked about. He kept that pain and its associated loss locked tightly in its box, but Monty's question banged on the sides of that box, weakening it and him.

"I've met your father and have an opinion of him. What's your mother like?"

"She's my mother," Hunter answered. Truthfully he'd never given her a great deal of thought. "She was there for me and took care of me, as in she cooked and cleaned and all that. But she primarily raised my sisters. Looking back, it was a very weird arrangement. We were a family and still are, but yet we were rather divided. I think my parents love each other, but Mom took the girls to ballet and gymnastics classes, and my dad never missed a football practice or game. Sometimes my mom came, but my dad was always there. He threw the football to me and ran drills in the backyard for hours after he got home from work."

"So he thinks your success is his success?" Monty asked.

"I think so. He comes to all my games, but he also thinks he's entitled to come over to the house with his friends and have parties. Last year he went to a class reunion and borrowed my Porsche to go. He didn't tell me. He left his car in its place, so I knew where it had gone, but he thought nothing of taking it. In his mind what's mine is his, I guess." Hunter sighed. "I talk to my mom because she worries, but I treat her differently. She's someone special, if a little further away, I guess."

"I don't understand why you think you don't deserve to be cared for," Monty continued, probing him with his gaze. "Or is it the real you thing? Are you scared that if people see the real you they won't like what they find?"

"I don't know," Hunter answered truthfully. "I haven't spent hours analyzing myself. I don't think I'm really all that deep. I'm a football player. How much damn depth can there be?" He was trying to make light of it, but judging by Monty's chilly response, it didn't work.

"Don't play the dumb jock with me. It isn't attractive. I've seen how careful you are. I bet you have friends who got huge signing bonuses with their first contracts and went through the entire thing in months. And I'm also willing to bet you still have your first signing bonus in an account somewhere making money for you."

Hunter couldn't deny that his brokerage account was quite healthy. "Okay, maybe you have a point."

"I see you for you, and I like you for you. Is that so hard to understand? I don't particularly care if you play football or work in a car wash. What's important is the person, not the occupation. I know all those people yesterday and today treated you a certain way because of what you do. I suppose that's easy to get used to and to buy into."

"I don't show people the real me because off the field I'm dull as dirt. I'm never the life of the party, and I don't like to be around large groups of people. The guys in New York I knew, but I'd never throw a huge party and invite everyone I know and the friends of friends, because I'd freak out with that many people in my house. Things happen at parties like that, unintended things, that can change everything in an instant." God, he needed to back away from the precipice.

"It's all right to want privacy. And you're entitled to have your secrets, but all I'm saying is you don't need to play that role with me." Monty lowered his gaze and rested his head on Hunter's chest. It took him a few seconds to realize Monty was trying to comfort him. He tried to remember the last time someone had done that. His father was a "buck up, be strong, don't cry, work through it" kind of guy. His idea of comfort was a beer and finding someone's ass to kick.

Hunter held Monty in return, smelling his hair and the remnants of the herbal shampoo he'd used. It was nice, and he was ready to get him home where it was quiet and they could be alone. Hunter wasn't sure what was going to happen, but excitement was already building after remaining on a slow simmer for the entire trip home.

"WHAT THE hell?" Hunter asked, leaning out the window when they approached the house. The driveway was full of cars, and he groaned. The limousine pulled up to the curb, and the driver let them out. Hunter only released Monty when he had to, but the desire and heat were now replaced with annoyance and a clear case of what the fuck.

The driver got their luggage, and Monty thanked him and made sure he knew where the bill should be sent. Then Hunter grabbed his bag and trudged up to the house with Monty behind him. He pushed open the door to a mess.

"Dad," Hunter called.

"In here." The television was on loud and every seat was filled. The dining room chairs had been brought in, and food covered the table and counters. It looked like some frat party had been going on in there.

"What's going on?" Hunter demanded.

"It's just a party," his dad said. "Come on in and grab a seat."

Hunter grabbed the remote instead and turned off the television. "Get the fuck out of my house, all of you. *Now!*" He glared at his father. "I didn't give you permission to be here."

"Now listen here, boy." His father jumped to his feet.

"All of you get out. I hope you had fun, because this is the last time. No more old-fuck parties at my house. You can go make a pigsty of your own homes, but not mine any longer. Go. Monty, call the police if this place isn't spotless and they aren't gone in five minutes."

"Boy, I made you who you are, and so help me—"

"Don't go there, Dad." He felt his resolve breaking. "I've had it. And tomorrow I'm having all the locks changed to be safe. So there will be no more parties or car borrowing or anything else like that. You want something, you can ask, in advance. This is not your home, it's mine." He calmed down somewhat. "You all need to go home, but you'll clean up your mess or so help me, I'll send you all the bill."

"You can't do this to me after what I did for you," his father growled.

"Look what you did for me. I was in New York working for two days, and you made one hell of a mess." He waved his arms all around.

"You should all be ashamed of yourselves," Monty said as he snapped pictures. "These are so I can send them to your wives. Let them know how you've been acting."

"Jesus," one of the men said. "She'll kill me." He grabbed a trash bag and began throwing everything away. One of the other men found the vacuum and got to work as well. Soon a dozen men were cleaning like mad and muttering how sorry they were while Hunter's father stewed and simmered away standing in the middle of the room with his fists clenching and unclenching, like a volcano ready to blow.

His dad narrowed his eyes as he turned toward Monty. "You keep out of this! You're the one who started all this. I know it. And don't fucking think for a minute that I don't know you switched off the power the other day. You think I'm dumb?" He stuck out his chest, glaring at Monty as he took a small step closer to him. His father was a master of intimidation, and he was pulling out all the stops. "You're only his assistant, and what the hell are you going to do when he wakes up and cans your pansy ass?"

Hunter was about to step in, but Monty took his own step forward, glaring back at his dad and standing as tall as his smaller stature would allow. "At least I respect him." Not only had Monty backed him up, but he was staring down his dad. "I can outstare my sister, and we once went at it for three hours straight, so unless you want to be here until the wee hours of the morning, I suggest you knock it off." Monty crossed his arms in front of his chest and then began tapping his foot impatiently. Hunter's dad became unnerved and turned his wrath back to Hunter. He could deal with that.

"Go home, Dad. I don't want to see you right now." Hunter turned away from his father. It was hard, but he was so angry, he'd hit him if his dad pushed further. "Regardless of what's going on in your head, you're the one in the wrong. So you can bluster and act like an ass all you want, but you're the one who behaved badly." Hunter stood by the door as the men left, saying they were sorry and hanging their heads.

"Those are my friends, and you treated them like they were dirt," his father said.

"No. You treated me and my home as if we were dirt, but that's over. Go home. I've had all of you I can stand for a while." He stared his father down and shut the door once his father had left. He leaned against the closed door, wondering what the hell he was going to do. In a matter of a few minutes, he had irreparably changed the relationship between him and his father. It was likely that his dad wouldn't speak to him for weeks, which was probably a good thing.

Hunter waited until his father drove away, in his own car, and then locked the door and turned off the outside light.

With Monty's help, it wasn't long before the house was back in reasonable order. "I'll have someone come in tomorrow and clean the carpets, and I'll go shopping because I'm assuming the plague of locusts ate everything in the house."

"Thank you." Hunter was worn out. He hadn't expected to come home to something like this, but he should have known. His father truly thought that Hunter's house was his to do with as he wished and that he could treat it like a garbage dump.

"Fucking hell, I'm tired and hungry." They hadn't stopped for dinner on the way home.

"I'll have something delivered for you if there's nothing in the fridge," Monty offered. "Go do what you need to, and I'll take care of things."

He was already digging in the fridge, so Hunter carried his suitcase up the stairs. He dealt with his clothes and cleaned up briefly. By the time he came back down, Monty had set up a place setting for him at the breakfast bar and had a plate ready.

"They left some things, so I heated you up some of the pasta from earlier in the week. I hope that's okay."

"What about you?" Hunter asked as he sat down.

"I'm going home."

"How? You need to get a new car."

"I know. I was going to ask if I could borrow yours for another day, or I can walk to the train station and ride home." Monty wiped the already clean countertops. "I should have kept my mouth shut."

"What are you getting at?"

"I should have kept quiet and cleaned up after your dad the other day. Things between you were none of my business, and because I brought things up and opened my big mouth, you and your dad are fighting." The cloth stilled.

"None of this is your fault. I wasn't happy about it, but I didn't know how to put a stop to it, and I should have a long time ago. My dad drives me crazy sometimes."

Monty sighed. "Like I said, I should have kept quiet. Then you could have dealt with this…. I know I pushed you into this." Monty set the cloth in the sink. "I'm going to get my bag and leave for the night. I'll be back in the morning. The train station is only half a mile away, and the walk will do me some good." Monty left the room, and Hunter stared at his food. It seemed every time they got close to one another, something happened to push them apart again. And it was driving him crazy.

Hunter pushed back from the breakfast bar, the chair legs scraping on the floor, and raced through the house. He caught Monty as he opened the front door. Hunter reached it and pushed it closed. When Monty turned to him, Hunter shoved Monty against the solid wood with his hips and chest, locking his gaze to his, and then leaned closer. "I want you, and I'm tired of letting things get in the way."

CHAPTER 8

MONTY STOOD still, afraid this chance would slip away as so many others had. The hard door pressed to his back as Hunter seemed to move in slow motion, getting closer, and Monty's anticipation rose higher and higher. He pressed his hands to Hunter's hard chest, closing his fingers in Hunter's shirt, needing something to hold as his knees threatened to buckle. Hunter hadn't even kissed him yet, and his legs were shaking.

Finally Hunter took his lips, demanding hard, with a force that said he wasn't going to stop and the damned house was going to fall down around them before he let Monty out of his arms.

Monty released his shirt and wrapped his arms around Hunter's neck, returning the kiss with as much energy as he was given. Monty hurt, he was so excited, and he wanted to adjust his cock to a more comfortable position, but that would mean letting go, and Monty had no intention of doing that for a second.

Hunter pressed to him more tightly, parting Monty's legs with a knee, grinding their hips together slowly. The hard rod pressed along Monty's, leaving no doubt as to what Hunter wanted.

"We're going upstairs to my room, and I'm going to strip you naked, get a good long taste of you, and then I'm going to fuck you hard." Hunter sucked at the base of his neck, with Monty stretching to give him access. "Is that what you want?"

"Oh God."

"If it's not, you need to tell me now." Hunter's deep tone rumbled through Monty. He'd wanted this, but doubt and what he thought he should do had warred with what he wanted for so damn long, he couldn't stand it any longer. "Is that what you want?"

"Yes," Monty hummed, and Hunter opened the buttons of his shirt one at a time, parting the fabric. Monty wanted to get the damn thing off, but the door was in the way.

"Leave your hands where they are," Hunter growled when Monty released them to work at his shirt. Once Monty's arms were around his neck again, Hunter lifted him off the floor, his big hands on Monty's ass. Monty wrapped his legs around Hunter's waist, and then Hunter turned and headed for the stairs.

"I can walk," Monty said, but Hunter kissed his words away as he climbed.

"You're not getting away this time," Hunter told him as they neared the bedroom. He took him inside, kicked the door closed, and laid Monty on the bed, pressing him into the mattress.

Hunter's solid weight was sexy, and his hands roamed over Monty's side and chest before sliding to his shoulders and pushing his shirt down and off. Monty shivered, but not with cold, as Hunter backed off a bit and proceeded to strip him of the rest of his clothes. This was no gentle, careful disrobing. Hunter was forceful, hands shaking a little, and Monty loved that he could do that to the much stronger man.

Once Monty was naked, Hunter pulled off his shirt, toed off his shoes, and removed his pants, and stood naked in front of him in all his hard-muscled splendor. Monty sat up, and when Hunter came closer, Monty held up a hand to stop him. Planes of muscle covered his chest, as perfectly sculpted as any classic marble statue. The wide shoulders and narrow hips he'd seen that first day. The long, thick cock that had been hinted at in so many near misses now pointed directly at him as though Monty were what Hunter wanted most.

But what caught Monty's attention was something he hadn't noticed before and he should have. Maybe his mind had been too caught up in the overall sight to truly think about it before. Hunter had a tattoo on his left shoulder.

"What's that?"

"Not now," Hunter answered and stalked closer, sending ripples of excitement through Monty. He quickly forgot about the ink as Hunter pushed him back onto the bed and slid his hands up from Monty's knees, along his quivering thighs, and then over his side and chest. He settled ever closer until his cock nestled beside Monty's throbbing one.

Monty thought he was going to come right there and had to think unsexy thoughts to stop it. Hunter lifted him, positioned Monty on the bed with his head on the pillows, and then kissed him hard enough to make his head spin. He'd had lovers before, well, a few, but none of them had made Monty want to forget everything and everyone.

"Are you going to do what you promised?" Monty asked.

Hunter chuckled deeply, richly, sending another wave of heat through him. Hunter answered by latching his lips on to one of Monty's nipples. He nibbled and then sucked and licked as Monty mashed his chest to Hunter's lips. He wanted more, and Hunter gave it to him, scraping his teeth lightly, driving Monty wild with the exquisite mixture of pleasure and pain. There was only so much exploration he wanted to do on the pain front, but the slight scrape was exactly what he liked.

"You're—"

"If you say cute or some other diminutive, I'm going to slap you," Monty warned.

"Why? You are cute."

"I want to be sexy, even virile, but cute... no guy wants to be cute. Especially when he's naked, if you know what I mean."

Hunter didn't answer, and Monty growled but stopped midbreath as Hunter licked down his belly and sucked just above his belly button.

"I said I was going to taste you, and I won't call you cute." Hunter ran his hands over his hips and then down to the base of Monty's cock. "Okay, how about this. The rest of you is cute, but this—" He licked up Monty's shaft and blew warm air on the head.

"—this is exquisite." Hunter groaned and then slid his lips over the head and down the shaft.

"I can live with that." Monty whimpered and thrust his hips forward, driving his cock deeper into Hunter's mouth. He pulled away quickly, not wanting to be too demanding or hurt him. "Jesus."

"Hmmm…," Hunter hummed around his dick, cupping his balls and teasing just behind them.

God, there was no way Monty could hold in the long, low moan that escaped his lips. "Hunter…."

"It's been a while, but I'm glad I still remembered how to do that." Hunter seemed pleased with himself, while Monty wanted to ask why it had been so long. Hunter could have any man he wanted. All he had to do was crook his finger and every gay guy for miles around would beat a path to his door. He had so many questions, but they would have to wait because Hunter had promised him a fucking, and Monty was on the edge just thinking about it.

"Do you have supplies?" Monty asked, saying a silent prayer that he did. Hunter pulled open the drawer near the bed and took out a string of condoms.

"I was hopeful," Hunter said, and Monty's eyes widened as Hunter kept bringing out more.

"Hope is one thing. That's…." Monty didn't know what the hell that was. "What did you do, buy out the entire drugstore?"

"I wasn't sure what kind you liked."

Monty grabbed one and handed it to Hunter. "This will do just fine." He kissed him, pulling Hunter's attention away from the safe-sex buffet and onto him. "You need to get me ready."

Hunter nodded, lifted and parted Monty's legs, then buried his face between them. That hadn't been exactly what Monty had meant, but Hunter went right at it, sucking, probing, teasing him enough Monty forgot everything other than the magical way Hunter made him feel. It was like every part of him held joy for Hunter, and he'd be damned if he was going to stop him. Hunter's attention and care made him feel special and warm. Yes, he hoped this would be more than just a passing fancy on Hunter's part, but Monty had few illusions. He would take what Hunter offered, happily.

"I want you, Monty," Hunter whispered when he lifted his head, his expression dark and his eyes swirling with passion. He brought his lips to Monty's, and Monty tasted himself on them, mixed with Hunter, and he knew that was perfection. "I think I have since that first day when your eyes practically bugged out of your head when I answered the door."

"You did that on purpose?"

"Of course not. But I saw the way you looked at me. People want to be me all the time and they want to have what I have, but you wanted me. You didn't even know who I was. You just wanted me, and now you can have me."

Hunter opened the condom and fumbled a little as he put it on. Then he got a small bottle of lube. Monty hissed when Hunter applied the slick to him. It was cold, but Hunter's touch warmed him quickly, and soon Monty was ready.

He groaned as they joined, Hunter sliding deep inside, filling him in a glorious combination of stretch, a flash of pain, and then nearly overwhelming heat and quivering lust. He wanted Hunter more than he needed to breathe.

As Hunter sank deeper, he placed his hand on Monty's chest. "I can feel your heart."

"Me too." Hunter's cock throbbed with each beat. "Take what you want, Hunter."

"I only want what you're willing to give."

Monty locked his feet behind Hunter's hips, tightened his grip, and pulled them closer and Hunter deeper. Shaking and trying like hell not to lose control, he groaned as Hunter slid over the spot inside him. It was too soon for this to be over, and Monty wanted Hunter's blue eyes to look at him and his hands to stroke him for as long as possible. "Then take it all and leave nothing."

Hunter groaned in Monty's ear, sucking on it as he undulated his hips. Then Hunter loomed up, big, strong, his chest full of power.

110

He held Monty's hips and drove forward with such force that Monty shook like he was having his own personal earthquake.

"Yes! I'm not going to break. I want you. Make me feel your power and strength." Monty grasped his cock, stroked as he watched Hunter come undone, sweat breaking out on his chest. The look in Hunter's eyes became feral as instinct and need took over. Monty clenched his muscles, gripping Hunter, determined to send him over the edge.

Monty felt the moment Hunter let go, and he held on to him to keep his head from banging on the headboard. Hunter was like a machine, driving into him, but he never took his gaze from Monty for a second. At times it was nearly overwhelming being the object of someone else's intense attention for so long, but it sent searing heat through him that stoked the embers of his passion to a roaring flame.

"That's it. God." The sensation of surrounding Hunter, his intense gaze, the tense and release of Hunter's muscles, the glistening sweat, and the heady scent of man all conspired to break Monty's control as he stroked himself and came so intensely he forgot where he was. Hell, for a few seconds, he fucking forgot his own name.

He opened his eyes, because he hadn't been able to keep them open, just in time to watch as Hunter tipped over the edge. His lips parted in a silent cry, and then Hunter threw his head back, chest and stomach tensing as he stilled, coming inside him.

Monty tugged Hunter down on top of him, held him as they shook through his release and stilled into the warmth of afterglow. He was in no hurry to move and groaned when Hunter moved. Still, they were going to stick to each other if they didn't clean up, and Hunter padded to the bathroom, removed the condom, and returned with a cloth and towel. He wiped Monty up and dried his belly before tossing the towel and cloth into the bathroom and then getting back into bed. Immediately Hunter held him but was stone silent.

Monty wondered if he should say something, but if Hunter didn't want to talk, he didn't want to break the mood for him. He lay there, soaking in the warmth and making slow, small circles on Hunter's chest. It wasn't until he raised his gaze from the acres of honey skin to Hunter's face that he got the shock of his life. Hunter was as close to tears as a strong, proud football player was likely to ever get.

Should he say something, or was it best if he remained quiet? Monty wished to hell he had an answer to that question. He lowered his gaze and decided to give Hunter his privacy. Hunter tightened his hold, clinging to him as though he might fly apart.

"Do you want to tell me?" Monty asked, breaking his silence. "You don't have to if you're not ready."

"No. It isn't embarrassing, it's just hard to talk about," Hunter said after a few minutes. "I know I told you it's been a while since I was with someone… like this. I was in college and I was seeing Michael. He was on the team with me. I was first string and he was third string, so he rarely got to play other than in practice. But he was good. Michael just lacked confidence." Hunter paused. "To make a long story short, we started working together, and he did better. When I sprained my ankle during a game, he came in and completed some key passes. It was awesome."

Monty liked that Hunter apparently had taken delight in his friend's success rather than worrying Michael would take his place on the team because he'd been hurt. That showed he was a good person. He didn't ask what happened and let Hunter say what he wanted. But Monty stopped stroking and let his hand rest over Hunter's heart. He wanted that connection to him.

"He and I spent a lot of time together after that, and after I was playing again, we did a lot of things, and one thing sort of led to another. I had the feeling that Michael was gay, and one night I got the confirmation. We ended up in bed. There was a whole lot of fumbling and not much else, but that broke the ice, and for the next few weeks, things were hot and steamy." Hunter grew quiet again, and Monty wondered if he was going to go on.

"I was living off campus at Penn State, and Michael moved into the house. Things were great—I had a friend, and we were together and having regular sex. It was awesome, and I started developing deeper feelings for him. Then his family found out that there might be more between us than just friends. I think one of our roommates might have said something accidentally."

"Did he leave school?"

Hunter continued without acknowledging Monty's question. "Michael didn't have a chance. His father said that he was coming up to see him and straighten him out. Michael was in a near panic and didn't sleep for two days. He was up wandering the house all night long. I tried to get him to calm down, but it wasn't going to happen. His dad was coming on Saturday, and I was supposed to go see my parents. I asked Michael if he wanted me to stay, but he said it would be best if he talked to his dad alone. Michael was calm and quiet that morning, and I thought he'd come to the conclusion that he was his own man and that it didn't matter what his dad said. So I left and got only about twenty minutes out of town before I called Mom and Dad and said I wasn't coming as I headed back to the apartment. I just couldn't let Michael face his dad alone."

"Had you told your mom and dad by that point?"

"Yeah. Dad had said he would support me, but that I should keep quiet until I was drafted. Mom had hugged me and told me she loved me. It was a moment when I think we were closer to each other than we had been in a long time. Anyway, I raced back. Everyone was supposed to be gone except Michael, so I ran in, glad his dad hadn't arrived yet, and hurried up the stairs. I nearly ran into him when I raced onto the landing. The house was a big old Victorian, and the stairs made a circle with supports that used to hold a chandelier of some sort at the top. Michael had strung a rope over the supports and hung himself. I think he'd jumped off one of the higher stairs, and it broke his neck."

"Jesus." What else could Monty say? His heart went out to Hunter at finding his friend and the guy he cared for like that, and then

113

he wanted to cry for Michael. To be that afraid of who he was that it was easier to kill himself than to face it…. That kind of self-hate was foreign to Monty because he'd figured out who he was early, but it was also familiar at the same time. He'd encountered it on more than one occasion.

"Apparently he intended his father to find him. I called 911 and left him alone. There was nothing I could do. It was obvious he was already dead." Hunter released him from the hug, pulled away, and stared up at the ceiling. "Michael's parents arrived just before the police and ambulance, and his dad fell apart. I expected him to be angry, but he stood in the living room, crying like a baby. He said he'd been angry when he'd first heard but had come to tell Michael that it was okay and that he understood and would stand by him. Michael's mother needed to be sedated, and I don't know how they made it through it."

"Oh my God. He was afraid of them and killed himself and it was for nothing. They…." Monty couldn't breathe. "That's so sad." He rolled onto his side to face Hunter. "Is that why you were so resistant when I first arrived?"

"Yeah. Since Michael, I haven't had anyone else in my life in a romantic way, and I thought if I had a woman assistant, there wouldn't be any tension. What I hadn't expected was to have this spitfire walk in my house and pretty much take over the emotional part of my life without me even realizing it. See, I blamed myself for Michael's death. I should have known that as upset as he was that he wouldn't have been so calm. When I talked to one of the team doctors, he said at that point it was likely that Michael had made up his mind and that's why he was calm."

"How could you have understood?"

"Doesn't matter. After Michael died, I came out to the coach and to the rest of the team. I wasn't going to hide any longer. Some of the guys said they had pretty much figured it out. A few weren't comfortable and always changed in another area of the locker room and even went back to their rooms to shower after practice, but I figured that was their choice."

"Did the team do something to remember Michael?"

"Yeah. They retired his number and held a service of healing for the entire campus. They took the whole thing as a chance to really try to help others. But I didn't see it that way and kept to myself. For the rest of the season, I threw myself into football, and then that summer and the next year I was determined to make it. Nothing else mattered. I had a few guys who said they were interested, but I was distant and kept working. I guess I made the pros and kept on that same path until you."

"So Michael was your only guy before me?"

"No. I had a few encounters, but they were cold, I guess you could say. It was just sex and nothing else. I didn't want to do anything to jeopardize my chances in the draft. Being gay was one thing. It had been done before and people were more accepting the second time around. But being a gay man out on the prowl and having my life paraded in the news was going to put people off, so it was easier to just keep to myself."

"Until now, when someone took pictures of us in the park," Monty said. He was still worried that was going to hurt Hunter somehow.

Hunter tugged him closer. "I'm tired of living my life according to other people. They can't expect me to be a saint forever. I'm a good player, and I make things happen on the field. The guys know that and so does the team management."

"Yeah, but what about the fans, and what if it becomes common knowledge that you're color-blind? The league could say that you aren't healthy enough to play. Then your career is over right then and there, and they won't need an excuse to sideline you." God, there were so many things that could go wrong. "How did you pass the physical?"

"I knew what the test was and gave them the answer they were expecting. No one said anything more about it. I never talk about colors, and I work so hard to compensate. I know the number of each player and design of every uniform worn by every team. Where their patches are, the size and shape, every detail. I can identify a team member just by that. I don't need to see the color of a uniform coming at me because I know who they are in an instant. Hell, I know the roster of each team and the number of each player."

"And yet you aren't able to read very well. Hunter...." Monty stroked his cheek. "You're smarter than you give yourself credit for. You work hard to overcome your challenges, so you can do this—can read—if you want to." Monty leaned in to kiss Hunter and then began to get out of bed. He hated to leave Hunter, but he needed to go home.

"You're going to leave?" Hunter asked with a hint of a pout that had Monty smiling.

"I have to go home because I don't have any clean clothes, and if I don't go home, my sister is going to give me complete hell." Like she wasn't going to do that as it was. "I'll be back tomorrow." Monty was already trying to figure out how he was going to get here. He needed to buy a new car, that was for sure, and he needed to find one he could afford. He'd decided he wasn't going to use Hunter's any longer. He could get used to the comfort and drive of the BMW, and what he was going to be able to afford was far from it. Also, with this latest development in their relationship, he was going to make damn sure he didn't take advantage. There had to be limits.

"Fine." Hunter lunged for him, and Monty squeaked and laughed as Hunter dragged him back down onto the bed, wrapped him in strong arms, and pressed him to his hard chest. "I'll just keep you here."

Monty settled in for a while, but time continued marching forward, and the grumbling of their stomachs brought them back to reality. Monty got up and dressed while Hunter shrugged on a robe.

In the kitchen a few minutes later, Monty took care of the food Hunter had left in his haste. That thought made Monty smile as he tossed the contents of the plate and made up a fresh one for him.

"You sit here and finish this one," Monty chided lightly. "I'm not going to have your teammates or coaches scolding you because you're losing weight… or whatever it is that they do."

Hunter chuckled. "You really have no idea."

"Not a clue. But I know they want you to keep up your strength. So eat, and I'll be back sometime in the morning unless you need me sooner." Monty walked around the breakfast bar, and Hunter snatched him, pulling him to his robed body. It would have been so easy for Monty to slip his hands under the robe. In fact, his fingers itched to touch, but he had to go or he was never going to get home. As it was, it was going to take well over an hour. Monty closed his eyes and leaned his head on Hunter's chest. He was so tempted to say screw it and stay. "I'll see you in the morning."

"Look, just take the car. If you have to leave, I want you to be safe. You can look for a new one tomorrow." Hunter went to the bowl where he kept his keys and returned to press them into Monty's hand. Then he leaned in and kissed him. "If you have to go, then do it before I take you back upstairs."

Monty nodded, got his bag, and left through the garage before he changed his mind.

MONTY FOUND a place to park under a light and walked up the stairs to the apartment, carrying his bag. He heard the yelling as he reached the top of the stairs.

"You could help, you know."

He knew that voice and that tone, and it sent a chill up his back. He wanted to turn around and go back the way he'd come. Taking a deep breath, Monty opened the door and stepped inside. The arguing instantly ceased as Em and his mother both turned to him from where they faced off in the center of the living room.

"What's the yelling for?"

"Your sister says she doesn't have time to help me. I need to go through some things at the house—"

Monty put his hand up as the acrid scent of resentment filled the room. "Mom, we don't live there any longer. So we aren't picking up after you anymore." This was an old argument. Very old. Their mother still felt that her children should help her around the house. He wondered if she'd taken her medication.

"But I can't do it alone." She rubbed her hands along the leg of her jeans. It was one of the nervous things she always did when she felt overwhelmed.

"Why not?" He could have been mean, and the words were on the tip of his tongue, but he bit them back. She was still his mother, and he didn't want to hurt her. "There's no one there but you to make the mess, so you need to pick up after yourself."

"But that will cut into her 'lying in bed and doing nothing' time," Em snapped, checking her watch.

"Is Camille working late tonight?"

"Yes."

"And I may have a job for you. I know someone who needs your help." Monty was being evasive on purpose. "We can work out the specifics later." He needed to get out of this room. First thing, if Camille came home and found Em this upset and angry, she was going to blow her top, and Monty did not want to be there when Camille went batshit crazy on their mother. She had done it before in defense of Emily, and Monty was grateful Emily had that kind of support, but he felt compelled to stand up for his mother, even though he didn't agree with her. And then things would turn ugly and Monty would feel like a doll being pulled in two different directions, and he just didn't need that shit. He had enough on his mind as it was.

Monty made it to his room before he heard voices raised once more. "I did what I could for both of you."

"Mom, a one-way trip down your birth canal does not equate to a lifetime of indentured servitude."

Monty nearly doubled over and had to put his hand over his mouth to keep from laughing. "That's enough, Mom. You need to be nice," he called from his room. "This is our home, and we have our own rules, and one of them is that you clean up after yourself. So leave Em alone. She's busy."

"Not that busy. She only works half days. She should be able to help."

Monty sighed. He hated that argument. Like what their mother wanted was so important that everyone should rearrange their schedule for her.

Monty clenched and shook his fists at the air. "She is busy and that's enough. You want to wallow in your own crap, then do so, but that is no longer our problem or responsibility." He was getting a headache. Monty closed the door and unpacked his bag, putting his dirty clothes in the hamper and figuring it was time to do laundry. At least the raised voices had quieted.

When Monty returned to the living room, his sister and mother were staring at each other.

"Did you have dinner?" Monty asked.

"Not yet." It was late, but Em liked to wait for Camille. Eating meals together was a big deal for them as a couple.

"Then I'll make something." He needed to keep busy because he was really beginning to wonder why he hadn't stayed with Hunter.

"I should be going," his mother said and stood. Monty hugged her tightly. She drove him crazy sometimes, but she was still his mother and he loved her. Em walked their mother out, and Monty hoped they'd take the chance to make peace between them. Monty went into their tiny kitchen and got to work.

"So I thought you were going to be home earlier?" Emily teased as she joined him. The tension that always accompanied a visit from their mother was forgotten until the next one.

"Things happened," Monty said.

"What kind of things, and don't leave anything out. Did he kiss you?" Emily gasped. "You did more than that, you have a bruise on your neck. You slept with him while you were gone." Emily slapped him on the back. "He's your boss."

"I know. And he's a great guy, and I really like him, and I guess he likes me. But I'm still confused. We spent most of the day

Sunday together in the park, where Hunter taught me some things about football."

"Yeah, I saw what he was teaching you. The picture was on display at the supermarket."

"Nothing happened, at least not then. He was just teaching me football, and when he ended up tackling me, some guy snapped a picture." Monty tried not to think it was the kid Hunter had signed the football for. That would really suck.

"So something has happened?" Emily teased.

"A lot happened while we were gone." He pulled out one of the stools and Emily sat down. "I need you to come with me to work and talk to Hunter. He doesn't read very well. The guy is smart, really smart, but he needs some help." Monty got lettuce and veggies out for salad. "He's spent a lot of years hiding his inability. No one really cared if he could read as long as he could play. So in high school and college, no one ever showed an interest." Monty grabbed the cutting board from above the refrigerator. "You also need to know that he's color-blind to a degree."

"He really wants help?"

"I think so. He's scared because his pride isn't going to let him ask for it, not really. But I said that you were a teacher and that you could help him, and he sort of agreed to meet you, so I think that's a step in the right direction."

"Wow, he has some issues. Is that why he was a dick at the beginning?" Em never pulled any punches.

"Part of it." Monty wasn't going to share the rest of what Hunter had told him. That was private.

"I'll be happy to meet with him. It isn't like I'm getting a bunch of job offers at the moment, and maybe some private tutoring would help bulk up my résumé." Emily was having a devil of a time finding a job after graduating with a degree in elementary education. The ones she'd been offered hadn't lasted long and so she was trying to make ends meet with subbing, which meant she had to be available at a moment's notice. Nothing ever seemed to come easily for either of them.

"It would also be a good thing to do. But you have to keep quiet about it. He's a proud guy, and I promised that you wouldn't tell anyone about that or the color-blind thing. It could get him in trouble with the league."

"What could?" Camille asked as she came into the apartment. "I see our wandering boy has returned home." She joined them, carrying a bottle of juice that she'd opened, and Monty distributed glasses. "And from the look on your face, someone got lucky."

"How do you two do that?" Damn, he couldn't keep the smile from his lips.

"Easy, you're moving funny," Camille said just before she and Em burst into laughter.

His backside was a little sore, but that was to be expected after ending a sexual drought of nearly two years.

"Hey, I don't say things about your sex life." Hell, he didn't *think* about their sex life. That was somewhere he didn't want to go.

"Yeah, but neither of us is having sex with our boss," Camille said. Monty knew she was teasing, but the comment hit too close to home, and he returned to his task. "Hey, I was only joking. He's a handsome man." Camille came around him. "You're a great guy and you deserve someone special."

"But he is still my boss, and things could get bad for him if it comes out. You can tease me, but what will people or the league say when they find out?"

"Sweetheart, we're only teasing you."

"But I slept with my boss," Monty said, taking a healthy swig of the grape juice.

Camille leaned over the counter. "Did you do it to get ahead or to make him give you the job?"

"God no."

"You really and honestly like him and you don't expect anything out of that other than his care and feelings in return."

"Of course. I would never do that." Monty emptied the glass and set it on the counter. But it sure as hell felt like he did, and he wished it didn't. When they had been together, everything was great, but now he was home and Hunter wasn't there, so all those questions in the back of his mind popped into his head.

"Then stop worrying. You're a good guy, and you'd never hurt anyone." Camille hugged him, patting him on the back, and then sat next to Em. The two of them did their lovebird thing.

Monty put on some rice and then made a stir-fry, the kitchen filling with the savory scent, and he tried to let his concerns float away, but it didn't work.

When it was time to eat, he made up plates for each of them. Then he refilled his glass and went to the other room to leave the two of them alone. They got so little time together, and he wanted them to have that. Someday he'd have someone to spend that kind of time with.

IN THE morning he drove back to Hunter's house to get to work. Thankfully it was quiet with no visitors. Hunter wasn't in the house, and Monty figured he was out on his run or at the gym. Monty went right to the office and checked both of their e-mail accounts. There were plenty, and he worked his way through them. When he opened the second to last one, he could hardly believe his eyes, and the words seemed bigger than life as his blood ran cold.

Monty picked up the phone and called Helen. "I need to speak to Garvin, please."

"What's wrong?" Helen asked.

"Hate mail. Hunter got hate mail today, and it was really nasty. I don't know if I should call the police or not." He couldn't take his eyes away from the evil missive.

"It's all right. We keep a file of them, and I'll go in and move it off so we have a record. I'll also make sure Garvin knows. But unless there's a specific threat, he's a public figure, and these come in from time to time."

"Okay." He closed the e-mail and left it in the account. It was freaky to have someone he cared for threatened like that.

"Don't worry about it."

"It's hard not to," Monty said as he heard the front door open and close. Then Hunter appeared in the doorway, his sweaty shirt clinging to his chest and his shorts gripping his beefy legs.

"It's hard not to what?" Hunter asked. He wondered if he should say anything. "You're pale."

"Helen, I have to go." Monty hung up.

"What's going on?" The smile fell from his lips.

"You got a piece of hate e-mail, and I was asking Helen what to do with it." He hadn't even wanted to tell him, and he felt so bad that he had to.

"Oh," Hunter said, shrugging his shoulders.

"You aren't upset? They said some really nasty things about you."

Hunter came into the office and sat in one of the desk chairs. "I'm a professional football player who's gay. There are people out there who don't believe I should be allowed to do what I love to do. They say I'm not good enough, or because I'm gay, that I'm not worthy to live or some such crap."

"Okay."

"Look. I love that you feel bad for me. Actually that's sweet of you. But please don't read it and don't take it to heart. I've gotten hundreds of them, and I know what the first one said, but I don't want to know any more. Helen and Garvin keep them in a file in case someone goes too far and then we can turn them over to the police."

"So you really do know." It hurt him that someone would say hateful, cruel things to Hunter.

Hunter nodded. "I need to go upstairs and get changed, but once I'm done, I thought we could try to find you a car."

Monty wasn't sure how much car he could afford at the moment, and it might be embarrassing to have Hunter going low-end used-car shopping with him. Still, it was nice of Hunter to offer to help.

"I have a few friends in the business, and they've agreed to help." Hunter stood and leaned over the desk. "I missed you last night. More than once I woke up thinking about you and wishing you were there."

"Me too." He felt a little dreamy as Hunter looked at his watch. "Is it break time?"

"I just got here an hour ago."

"Yeah, but is it time for a coffee break?" Hunter asked.

"Okay. I'll put a pot on." Monty hurried to the kitchen and started the coffee. Once the rich, earthy scent filled the house, he poured two mugs, one the exact way Hunter liked his, and went in search of the man himself.

There was water running upstairs in the master bathroom, so Monty knocked once on the door. The shower stopped. "I'm putting your coffee out here for you."

The door opened, and Hunter stood on the mat, naked, dripping water everywhere. "Since it's break time, I thought we could spend it together."

"Hunter," Monty said, his fortitude breaking way too damn fast. "We can't do things like this while I'm working. You're paying me to do a job, and I can't get my work done if I'm thinking of you... like this... all the time."

Hunter took both mugs, set them on the bathroom counter, and tugged Monty inside. "Sweetheart, you get a coffee break, so for the next fifteen minutes, you're all mine. No job, just me." Hunter pushed the door closed and pulled Monty's shirt over his head. Then he stripped off Monty's pants and socks after Monty managed to kick his shoes off. Hunter tugged him into the massive shower and turned on the water. Heat cascaded over him, and the space filled with steam. Hunter grabbed the soap and lathered up. "Turn around," Hunter whispered, and when Monty did, he pulled him back until his ass slid along Hunter's cock. Hunter's huge, strong hands slid around his waist to his belly. "Can I fuck you in here? Up against the wall?"

"Is that all you want? To fuck me?" Monty asked.

"No. I want to feel you around me, taste you." Hunter slipped his hands lower, gripped Monty's cock and cupped his balls with soap-slicked hands. God, the sensations that added. "I love the way you feel next to me. You're smooth, and while you're not hard, you're... perfect. I love the way you feel and how I feel when I'm with you."

"Hunter." Monty groaned as he sucked his ear, stoking Monty's desire to a near fever pitch.

"It's true, Monty. You make me feel like I can do anything." Hunter turned him, looked deeply into Monty's eyes, caressed his cheek before kissing him, sliding his tongue between Monty's lips. He sucked on it and let Hunter press him to the wall. "Stay right there." Hunter slid down until he was on his knees and at mouth level with Monty's cock. "You're an amazing man." To prove it, Hunter parted his lips and took him to the root.

"Hunter," Monty groaned, slapping the wall with his open hands. Hunter made him feel so alive and like he was the center of his universe. "Dang, you're so good at that."

"I like to throw myself into my work and my coffee breaks." He took him in again until Monty's knees shook. Then when Hunter pulled back, he turned Monty to the wall again and parted his legs.

"Hell...." Monty adored when Hunter rimmed him. He threw his head back, eyes peering up at the ceiling, and he wondered what in the hell he'd done to deserve being the focal point of this man's attention. "Hunter, please... fuck me."

Hunter turned off the water, pulled the door aside, and came up with a condom and lube. Hunter rolled on the condom, moved closer once again, and lifted Monty off his feet. "Put your legs around my waist and relax. I'm going to lower you onto my cock."

"Hunter, we could—" Hunter breached him, and Monty didn't care how awkward the position was anymore. His body relaxed and opened, wanting Hunter as badly as the rest of him.

"It's going to be fast, sweetheart," Hunter said and flexed his hips, pushing him back and forth. Monty held on as Hunter fucked him hard, one hand steadying his back and the other at the base of his ass to keep him from falling. Monty didn't think about it after a few seconds. All he wanted was Hunter inside him, kissing him, holding him. It was like he was at an open buffet and could have all the ice cream he could eat.

ANDREW GREY

"You feel amazing on my cock," Hunter growled.

"You just feel awesome. Now talk less and fuck harder." Hunter complied, and Monty's cries echoed off the walls of the confined space. He leaned back and Hunter went deeper, driving him completely wild. This was amazing, and as Hunter's movements became erratic, Monty held on tighter until Hunter spilled deep inside him.

He stilled, and Monty climbed down. Hunter kissed him and sank down to his knees to suck Monty once again. It only took a few seconds before he was on the edge. Monty gasped and gave Hunter as much notice as he could, but his release barreled into him, and he ended up pumping his load down Hunter's throat as lights sparkled behind his eyes.

Monty leaned against the wall, and Hunter pressed against him like a sexy, warm blanket. Hunter turned on the water and began to wash him again, this time slowly, carefully, and so gently. Monty didn't want to move. Being the object of someone else's intense attention was addictive and something he could get used to very easily.

"You're so damn special."

"Because we have sex?" Monty teased.

"Absolutely not. We have sex because you're special. You're the first man since Michael. You know that. And you've helped me heal. I never thought that would happen—that I could trust myself again."

"That wasn't your fault," Monty said as he moved out from under the water and Hunter washed his chest and down his belly.

"I know."

Then Monty stepped back under the spray, rinsing off the soap and reaching for the bar. He got behind Hunter, running his soapy hands over his wide back and then down to his tight bubble ass. He was firm and strong all over.

Hunter startled when Monty ran his soapy fingers down his crack.

"I want you too," Monty said, winding his hands around to Hunter's cock, which he cleaned very thoroughly.

"I've never done that," Hunter admitted.

"I didn't think so." He wasn't going to press him. He lay against Hunter's back, holding him and letting water cascade over the both of them. "It's all right. You're enough for me as it is."

CHAPTER 9

"I DON'T know what that word is," Hunter said with frustration as he and Emily sat at his kitchen table.

"I know," Emily, the taskmaster who was teaching him to read, responded lightly. Well, she'd been trying to teach him for the past week, though it didn't seem to be doing him any good. "This is an exercise in letting you see new things. Now just read the article and sound out any words you don't know." Emily was so patient.

Hunter looked over at Monty, who sat behind his computer, ignoring them.

"I can't."

"Sure you can. Just break the word down. I know it's large, but if you break it into smaller pieces, you can read it."

"Extr—ord-in-ary. Extraordinary," he read and smiled.

"See. You already know all these words—you just need to learn how to read them. Now go on and continue reading."

"But I sound dumb," Hunter said. At least he *felt* dumb, really dumb.

"No, you don't. You sound like someone who is learning, and you're doing well. Now continue reading the article."

"Em." Monty came over. "Let him try to read this." He took the page Hunter was holding and handed him a different one.

Hunter looked at it. "Hunter Davis, the wide receiver for the Philadelphia Red Hawks, has been announced as the newest spokesperson for Johnston Brands and will appear on a billboard in Times Square, with images to appear in many magazines and newspapers. This reporter was fortunate enough to get a sneak preview of the images to be used, and they are hot enough to make any woman buy her husband a drawer full of drawers." Hunter grinned.

"See, you can do it," Emily said, and Hunter felt Monty's hands on his shoulders.

"You just needed something interesting to read. I could buy you a few copies of a certain kind of magazine, and you could read some stories that you'll find very interesting." Monty's eyes were gleaming as he teased.

"That's enough of that." Emily reached into the bag she always brought with her and pulled out a few books and handed them to him. "I want you to read these. They're what we call midgrade stories, but they're at a reading level that you're at. It will help you feel more comfortable. Just like anything else, practice will get you more proficient. They won't take you long, and the stories will help you learn." Emily handed him the books and then excused herself, probably to use the restroom.

"I said you could do this," Monty whispered to him. "And once Emily is gone and we're done with work for the day, I'll give you your reward."

"I don't have any appointments today. Though tomorrow I'm busy all day in meetings and working with the coaches to make sure I haven't slipped during the off season."

"But you have homework, and once that's done, you'll get your reward." Monty kissed his ear.

"You're a mean one."

"I'm only mean if I don't deliver, and I will, you know that." Monty moved away as Emily returned, trailing his hands down Hunter's shoulder as he went.

"You're doing very well. Just keep practicing, and I'll have some more lessons and books for you the next time. I know you're going to get very busy, and interest in the upcoming season is going to start to reach a fever pitch. That's why I'm pushing so hard right now—so you can have a chance to make real progress before your life gets too busy."

"Thank you. You're an amazing teacher." Hunter walked her to the door and saw her out to her car. He watched her leave and was about to close the door when a familiar car breezed into the drive.

"Mother," Hunter said as she got out of the car. "I wasn't expecting you."

"This isn't a happy visit," she said as she stormed up the walk and into the house. Hunter closed the door. "I've had it with whatever is going on between you and your father."

"Excuse me?"

"For the last two weeks, I've been overrun by all his friends. Every Thursday they come over, spend the afternoon watching television, eat me out of house and home, and then leave like a herd of lemmings." That sounded like his father to Hunter. "When I asked him about it today, he said it was your fault. Because you kicked him out and won't let him do it at your place. Well, you and your 'assistant from hell.'"

Hunter chuckled as he motioned his mother toward the living room.

"What's all this?" she asked, picking up the books from the coffee table.

"I'm getting some help with my reading." Hunter found it hard to answer, but this was his mother and he felt he should be honest with her.

"All right, but this… it can't be that bad." She sat on the sofa, and Hunter took the nearby chair. "Bettering yourself is one thing…."

"Mom. I can read only simple things. A newspaper is difficult for me, if not impossible." Monty came into the room, and Hunter motioned him over. "Monty, this is my mother, Clarise. Mom, this is Monty, my assistant from hell."

"Excuse me?" Monty said.

"That's what my husband calls you. Apparently you put an end to his fun, and now I have to deal with it."

"I think you need to talk," Monty said, and he looked like he couldn't leave the room fast enough, though he didn't go.

"Please, sit down. That was rude of both of us," his mother said, and Monty sat in the chair across from her. "The thing is, he's driving me crazy. For years you've been the center of his attention. He took you to games, helped you practice, and then pushed and pushed until you were drafted, and now he thinks you don't want him around any

130

longer. And those damn friends of his are a bunch of posers who hang on to him because of who you are."

"He was disrespectful, Mom. I was out of town and he was here and made one hell of a mess. I know me being a football player is a big deal for him, but that's all he cares about."

"That's not true," she said, but Hunter shook his head.

"Mom, can the girls read and write? Because I'm what they call functionally illiterate. I'm learning and working hard. All Dad cared about was my playing football. Nothing else mattered. So pardon me if I'm a little angry with him at the moment because of the things I missed out on because he didn't give a damn." Hunter tried very hard not to be angry with his mother even though he knew she shared some of the blame.

"I'm sorry, honey," she said, wiping a tear away. "I honestly didn't know. Whenever I tried to step in, your father told me that you were his son and that he knew what was best for you." She opened her purse and pulled out a tissue. He knew how forceful and bullying his dad could be, but he was still saddened that his mother hadn't stood up for him. "But I don't know what to do. You have to make peace with him somehow." She sat back on the sofa, dabbing her eyes.

"I don't know if I can. I said some harsh things, but he needed to hear them. He's been out of control, and the things he said to Monty were completely uncalled for. Monty is my assistant, and he was looking out for my best interests when I wasn't able to be here. That's his job, and Dad treated him like he was his own personal servant. I can't have that." Hunter leaned forward. "Dad always said that when we were under his roof, we had to obey his rules. Well, this is my roof, and he needs to remember that."

"Your father is...." It was obvious that his mother loved his father even if she had a difficult time dealing with him. "I wish he and I had done things differently. I should have stood up to him a lot more and made sure that you were learning. I always thought Simon put too much emphasis on football and sports, but he wouldn't hear anything about it."

"I know that. The teachers didn't really care as long as I behaved in class and wasn't disruptive, and the few who did take an interest and tried to bring up what was going on were shouted down by Dad and the school officials because they wanted to win football games. That was all that mattered. So if Dad wants me to make peace with him, then he has to take the first step. I may have been angry with him, but he failed me in a much larger way." Hunter was tired of talking about this and left the room. He should have suspected that his dad would eventually send his mother to talk to him.

"He's hurt," Hunter heard Monty say. "I'm not here to get into the middle of his family business. I'm his assistant, not his counselor. But I like to think I'm also his friend, and Hunter needs some time. He's taking steps to improve himself, and that should definitely be applauded." He'd stopped to listen but then went into the kitchen. He was not going to eavesdrop in his own house. Hunter got something to drink for himself, Monty, and his mother, and returned to the living room. Monty left the room when he came in, saying he was getting snacks, and Hunter handed his mom a glass of iced tea.

"I don't want to talk about him."

"I know. But your father and I did a lot right with you." She drank from her glass. "Everyone makes mistakes, and there are some things I wish more than anything that I could take back. If I had the chance, I'd see to it that you and I had more time together. Your sisters and I used to go away every year as a mother-daughter thing, and we should have had a mother-son getaway too."

"We still can, Mom. If you want to do that, we can. Maybe we can go to the beach for a few days." He wasn't sure what they would do or what they had in common, but he was willing to find out. What shocked him was how little he really knew about his own mother. "What would you like to do? We can go anywhere and do anything you like."

His mother straightened up with a grin on her face that sent a chill of intrigue down his spine. "I want to ride horses and go on a hot-air-balloon ride, and after that I want to jump out of an airplane. If President Bush can do it at eighty, I think I can do it too."

Who would have thought his mother was a daredevil? "Okay, Mom, we'll do all those things. But let's start with the riding and hot-air-balloon ride. I don't think I'd dare jump out of a plane until my contract is up. My coaches, trainers, and agent may not survive it."

"Don't forget assistants," Monty said, carrying in a tray. He set it on the coffee table before leaving once again.

"He's something else," Hunter's mother said as she watched Monty leave the room, and then she turned her attention to him. "Is he more than your assistant? You follow him with your eyes whenever he comes near, and he touches you in that way just to let you know he's nearby."

"I guess we're figuring things out, Mom. Monty is a nice man who has my best interests at heart."

She nodded. "But do you have his best interests at heart?" Hunter thought that a strange question. "He's your assistant. If something happens to end things between you, he's the one likely to suffer. He'll lose someone he cares for and his job, and no matter what you say, that boy cares for you."

Hunter nodded. "What are you saying?"

"Look, your daddy raised you to be a number of things, and being self-centered comes with the territory of being a top-class athlete. You have to watch what you eat, train, and you always had your own schedule that never worked in with anyone else's."

"Are you saying I'm selfish?"

"Maybe a little. But you need to understand that in order to get where you are, you had to focus for years on your skills, practice, games, and then more practice. I remember Simon taking you to an indoor arena in February so the two of you could throw the ball and keep your skills sharp. Your focus was always on your skills and football."

"Yes, and it still is. I'm not going to let anything take my eye off the prize," Hunter said proudly.

"That's my point. Whoever you love deserves to be just as important in your life as football. There are going to be times when you will have to make choices, and football can't win each and every time." She reached across and patted him on the hand. "If you care for Monty, then eventually you're going to have to make some decisions about your life."

"But...."

"I know this is blasphemy to you, but the entire world isn't football. Sometimes there are other things that are more important."

"But I can only play for so long and then it's going to be over. Not everyone can play until they're into their forties like Brett Favre. I have to make the most of this while I can."

"Honey, I'm proud that you have a head on your shoulders and know the realities, but there is one just as important. Your football career may have a limited shelf life, but so does love, and it needs just as much care and dedication as the rest of your life."

Hunter wondered why they were having this conversation. Everything was really good in his life right now. He and Monty had sort of figured some things out. They had work hours, and during that time, they were professional, but once those hours were over, they were able to put the work aside and rock each other's worlds. The only problem was that Hunter wanted Monty to work less and spend more time with him. But he was being good and abiding by Monty's wishes. "I'm trying, Mom."

She finished her tea and got up to leave. "I have to get to the store and then back home before your father decides to have more people over." She grabbed her purse, which was big enough to hold everything she might ever need, possibly even to climb Mount Everest, and she walked to the door. Hunter hugged her good-bye and held the door for her. He waved as she got back in her car, and then closed the door. Once he'd locked up, Hunter went in search of Monty and found him in the office with the door closed.

"Did your mom leave?" Monty asked as he looked up from his computer. "You just got an e-mail from the coach. He's called a meeting for five o'clock tomorrow. He asked that everyone confirm, so I did and added it to your schedule."

"She did. Was there any indication what it was about?"

"No," Monty answered. "Though some of the other players might have an idea. I'm assuming there's a rumor mill of some sort. You could ask if you're concerned."

"Not really. I'll find out soon enough." Hunter stepped up to the desk, walked behind it, and leaned down. "I've been thinking about you the entire damn day."

"You have?" Monty smiled. "I have some work to finish up, and you have some homework you have to do, and after that we'll talk about your reward." Monty sat back in the chair until he was looking up at Hunter, eyes half-lidded.

"What kind of reward are we talking about?" Hunter placed a hand on each of the chair arms, leaning closer and closer to Monty. God, he was so damn lucky to have Monty in his life. He added joy and sunshine Hunter hadn't realized was missing.

"I don't know yet. While you're reading, I'll come up with something really special that you're going to love." Monty sat forward and kissed him heatedly, and Hunter pushed him back into the chair. All it took was a single kiss and Hunter was hard and raring to go. He wanted Monty so badly, with every fiber of his being, each and every time. Monty was like a drug and he was totally addicted.

"You need to get to work," Hunter growled and reluctantly left the office, got books and sat down to read. Though he wasn't sure how he was going to get anything done with Monty in the house.

"I have some errands to run," Monty said as he passed the doorway a little while later. "I need to pick up your laundry and go to the store. I'll be gone for a few hours." At least that took care of one distraction.

"I thought you went to the store yesterday."

"Go ahead and read. I'll be back." Monty left the house, and for the millionth time, Hunter wondered how he was going to get along if anything happened to Monty. In less than a month, Monty had become a fixture in his professional life. Hell, most people called to speak to him directly now. And Monty had become a staple in his bed, something Hunter hoped would never end. God, he was falling in love. As soon as the idea crossed his mind, he knew exactly what his mother meant. He wanted to spend time with Monty.

His phone rang, and Hunter answered it.

"You up for poker tonight?" Joe asked.

"Sure. Do you guys want to come here?" It was likely his turn.

"Great. I'll call the others and we'll see you at seven." Joe hung up, and Hunter messaged Monty to let him know what was happening and got a response that he'd get some snacks while he was out.

Do you play poker? Hunter messaged. *You could join us if you like.* Just like that Hunter realized that he could play poker with the guys or have Monty at the game as well and not spend the entire evening thinking about Monty and what he was doing. Damn, he really had it bad.

"I BET ten." Monty threw in his chips and sat back. Monty had exactly zero poker face. He smiled when he had something, and everyone around the table knew it. Not that it really mattered. He was having a good time with these guys from the team. Even Joe seemed to have let some of his reservations go. Of course the cheesecake and the cookies that Monty had baked and placed on the end of the dining room table might have had something to do with that.

"I'll see you and raise you fifteen," Mark said, tossing in his chips and snagging a cookie. "Dang, these are good. You have to give my wife this recipe."

"I don't think so, big guy," Hunter said, patting Mark's belly. "The coach and your wife are not going to be happy with what's going on here. It looks like you've already had one too many cookies."

"I've been dieting all damn week and working out like crazy, man. I need some food." He finished the cookie. Hunter folded, throwing in his cards. Monty continued smiling, and it was clearly unnerving Mark.

"Twenty." Monty tossed in his chips.

Mark groaned and buried his cards. "What did you have?"

"Gotta pay to see them," Monty said and winked at him. Hunter turned away, knowing Monty had just creamed them all with a spectacular bluff. Monty raked in the chips, doing a little swoopy-shoulder dance. Okay, maybe Monty had his own poker face after all. "While Mark deals, do any of you need anything else to drink?"

"I'll get them," Hunter said. "You aren't working tonight," he added to Monty and went into the kitchen for another round of beers. When his phone rang, he snatched it off the counter. "Hello."

"Mr. Davis, I'm with the *Inquirer*, do you have any comment on—"

"No." He hung up and set his phone down. He'd had it drilled into his head never to give comments over the phone to anyone. He made a note to contact Garvin in the morning so he could figure out what was going on. Hunter grabbed the beers and returned to the table.

"Dang reporters. They always call for some damn comment on something." Hunter passed out the drinks.

"Tell me about it. I change my number and the leeches get it again in a few days. I never answer calls from people I don't know," Joe said. "Go ahead and deal the cards."

Hunter shuffled, had Mark cut, and then Mark dealt. They bet around the table, with Monty smiling once again. Hunter was really starting to hate that smile and wondered what he was up to. Hunter was pretty sure he'd been bluffing the last time, but this one was accompanied by a twinkle in Monty's eyes. He was determined to ignore Monty and play the hand. They took their cards.

"I bet twenty," Monty said.

"Raise twenty more." Joe took a swig of beer.

Clyde called, and Randall folded. Hunter raised another twenty and turned to Monty, whose smile had faded a little.

Joe called and showed his cards. "Three aces," he crowed, and Hunter tossed him his cards.

"Full house." Monty grinned like an idiot as he pulled in the biggest pot of the night. "I can arrange a loan if you guys need it."

Hunter's phone rang from the kitchen, where he'd accidentally left it earlier. He rose and hurried in to answer it. He expected it to be another reporter call, but it was his mom.

"Hey, Mom, what's going on?"

"I'm sorry, honey…."

"What?"

"Your father went out to Brewster's, and he had too much to drink. I was called to come pick him up and… well… there was a reporter there. They wanted a quote about you and the fact that someone was helping you with your reading. Your father apparently did a lot of talking. The resentment that I talked to you about must have been on full public display."

"What did he say?" Hunter tried to figure out what the hell he was going to do. He steadied himself and tried his best not to let his imagination run away with him.

"I don't know exactly, to be honest. I put the old fool to bed, and he's sleeping it off, I hope. I doubt he'll remember what he said, but I thought you should know what happened."

"Thanks, Mom," Hunter said softly and hung up. So the phone calls were attempts by the reporter to corroborate their story. Of course no one would speak to them. But somehow he got the feeling it wasn't going to matter. Monty joined him in the kitchen where Hunter stood with his hands on the counter.

"What happened?" Monty asked.

"My father opened his mouth." Hunter looked up from the granite countertop. "Apparently he'd been drinking for a good part of the day, and there was a reporter asking about my not being able to read…. Mom doesn't know what he said exactly. She's got him in bed now, but she wanted me to know." God, this was going to turn into one hell of a mess. Just what he needed.

"I'm sorry," Monty said, sliding his hands around his waist and just holding him. "I know things with your dad aren't very good right now, but how bad could it really be?"

"You don't read?" Joe asked.

Hunter looked down, heat creeping up his cheeks. "Not well. Monty's sister has been helping me. You know how it was in school— no one cared as long as we played well."

"Shit yeah," Mark said. "Being a football player with troubles in school is like being a basketball player who's tall. A lot of us have that problem, especially if we came from an inner-city school where there were troubles to begin with. So you got some help—that's to be commended, not ridiculed." Mark pushed away from the table, and all the guys got on their phones, most likely to make sure they weren't getting calls at home.

"What are you going to do?" Randall asked him.

"I don't know what I can do. I mean, not being able to read well isn't something I'm proud of, but a story about how I'm trying to better myself isn't going to sell a bunch of newspapers either. Unless they're doing some human interest thing."

"It's the *Inquirer*. They're usually a good paper as far as I know," Monty said, and the guys nodded.

"It isn't some rag," Joe agreed.

"Who knows?" Hunter tried not to get too upset about the whole thing. But it was hard. There was something brewing, and this warning from his mom was the tip of the iceberg. If someone close to him had been talking to a reporter, then who the hell knows what they said?

CHAPTER 10

LORD, THE question he'd asked Hunter two days ago rang in his ears.

Hunter had been on the phone with Garvin and his publicists the following day, and apparently they had talked over many strategies for handling whatever fallout was to come. Monty had rescheduled his day, and of course Hunter had to go to his team meeting. Hunter told him he'd spoken with the coach afterward to let him know that something was coming, but now it was a waiting game to see what happened.

Monty had done his best to try to take care of Hunter and keep his mind on productive things, but it didn't seem to be working, so he'd ended up taking Hunter to bed multiple times, trying to keep his mind off it. Those had been screamingly intense times, which left Monty breathless and sore in the best way possible.

"Maybe this will blow over," Monty asked as he met Hunter at the bottom of the stairs after two days without anything in the news.

"I don't think so. Once they have their fingers in something juicy, or potentially so, they aren't going to let it go."

"But you'd think they'd write whatever it is they want to and get it over with." The waiting and uncertainty were the hardest part of this whole thing. Monty hadn't gotten much done in the last few days other than try to keep Hunter from going in every direction possible all at once.

"Today is Saturday, so if anything does happen, it will be tomorrow. The paper has its best circulation, and that's when whatever they want to say will gain the widest audience." Hunter sat down on the living room sofa with Monty taking the place next to him.

"I keep wondering what they could write about. So you and your dad had a fight—that's hardly front-page news. What else would he say?"

"You," Hunter said. "They could go after you somehow. God knows what my dad said. When I talked to him, he was so apologetic, but he swears he doesn't remember anything about what he said."

"So the reporter was talking to a drunk guy and is trying to use him as a source. That isn't going to be very reliable, and they're going to have to get more than that to put together a real story. They have to get their facts right. Maybe that's why it's been quiet. If no one else is talking, then they have no place to go with it." He was probably grasping at straws because he didn't know what they had, but he needed Hunter to feel better.

"Are you going to stay tonight?" Hunter asked, and Monty was so tempted to say that he would. He'd spent the last two nights nestled in Hunter's arms, trying to provide any comfort he could. The thing was he'd been the one comforted. Regardless of what happened or what was on the horizon, he felt safe and warm in Hunter's embrace.

"I need to go home. I don't have any clothes. But I will be back first thing in the morning if you need me." Monty kissed Hunter and stood. "I will scour the paper tomorrow and see if there's anything there." He hated to leave, but he hadn't been home in two days, and Em was going to think he'd left for good.

"Call me when you get there."

"I will, I promise. And you need to get some rest and not fixate on this all night. Garvin and your publicity people are on this as well. They will put out whatever they think they need to in order to counter whatever is coming. The thing is, the reporters made a mistake by tipping their hand like that, and now you can be ready."

"I know," Hunter agreed, and Monty gathered his things to get ready to leave.

"I'll be back in the morning. I promise." He leaned down, kissed Hunter one more time, and wished he could stay. "Em has invited Mom over for breakfast, and I need to be there to make sure they don't start going at it again." The breakfast would provide a chance at peace between the two of them.

"I understand." Hunter sounded clipped and tense. "I'll be fine."

141

"Are you sure?" Monty asked. "I could stay and get up really early to go back to Em's so I can be there when Mom gets there...." He bit his lower lip.

"It's Sunday. You don't need to do all that. I'll be okay, and you need to spend some time with your family. I'll see you in the morning." Hunter walked him to the door. They shared a kiss with the door closed, and then Monty left the house, got into his new-to-him silver Volvo, and drove home.

Monty continually glanced in the rearview mirror to see if he was being followed. Not that he was an expert on things like that, but the last few days had him spooked. Em had said she'd gotten another call but had said nothing and hung up. That had been yesterday, and since then, as far as Monty knew, everything had been quiet. He didn't see anyone behind him as he drove, though by the time he reached the apartment, he was jittery as hell. There were no parking spaces where they lived, so Monty circled until he got lucky when one opened up. He parallel parked and got out, hurrying up and inside like a scared rabbit.

"Have you heard anything more?" Em asked as soon as he entered the apartment. Camille stood right behind her.

"No." Monty put down his bag and hugged both of them. "Hunter is going crazy, and he's wound up tighter than a drum."

"Does he really have anything to worry about?" Camille asked as they moved into the living room. "He's a public figure, and things like this happen. Someone opened their mouth, and it put a bulldog reporter on his trail. They might find a story, but then they might come up with zip and all of this could be for nothing."

"I hope so." But his gut told him there was something more. Hunter had secrets he was keeping, but didn't everyone? "I mean, the things I know about shouldn't be a huge deal, except the color-blind thing if the league really would bar him because of something like that."

"Who knows? They could feel that he'd be a danger on the field."

"Please. He's lived with it his entire life. If anything, he should be commended for overcoming a challenge to playing and becoming one of the best players in spite of it." Monty shook his head slowly. "Whatever comes is going to be personal and mean-spirited. You know, like one of those sideline columns they write to stir things up or get people fired up about some cause or other."

"Still...." Camille motioned to the sofa. "Did you eat?"

"Yeah. I made dinner for Hunter and came home so I could make breakfast for this whole Mom thing in the morning, so maybe we can put this quarrel behind us. We are a family, after all, and I wanted to be here to help."

"You could have stayed and come before she arrives."

"Actually, it was Hunter who said I should come home. He didn't want me to have to get up so early tomorrow," Monty said, but he was still nervous about it. His mind kept going back to the story Hunter had told him about Michael and how he'd left and regretted it. Monty wished he'd stayed so Hunter wouldn't be sitting there alone. Monty sent him a message just to make sure he was all right, but he didn't get an answer.

I'm on my way back he sent as a second message and hurried to his bedroom to get some fresh clothes. Emily and his mother would have to work things out on their own. He had someone more important at the moment who was sitting alone, worrying.

His phone beeped. *Don't. Going to bed.*

Monty read the message more than once and then put down his phone. Hunter had made his feelings clear enough, and Monty would abide by it. He thought of calling him but decided to leave it.

"Okay," Em said when Monty showed her the message. "He's a big boy, and he knows what he wants."

Monty didn't have an argument for her and set his bag beside the doorway. Then he went into the bathroom, cleaned up, and went to bed but didn't sleep for hours. He worried for Hunter and for himself. No matter what Hunter said, whatever was brewing was going to be big—Monty knew it in his heart. Hunter's father knew every secret and had been so filled with hurt and bile that, Monty could imagine, with a little alcohol to loosen his lips, everything a reporter could want to know about Hunter probably came pouring out of him like water through a sieve. Monty kept coming back to the things he knew about Hunter, as well as what he didn't, and the revelations that could be included.

MONTY WOKE from a restless sleep and hurried out front to grab the Sunday paper from the lobby of the building. He checked over the front page while he carried it up and didn't see a story. He went inside and set the paper on the table, pulling off section by section until he came to Sports. He scanned it and didn't see anything at first. Then his eyes caught Hunter's name on a column, just like he'd said. "Hero No More," the title read, and Monty sat down to see what it contained.

By the time he'd finished the article, Monty needed a shower, but he was afraid to strip off his shorts and T-shirt in case he felt more exposed. The column talked about Hunter and how his father had supported him for years and how they'd had a falling out. But Monty was listed as the reason for the fight.

"Is that it?" Emily asked over Monty's shoulder, and he handed her the paper. His hands felt dirty just from touching it. "Jesus...."

"Yeah, and they don't even mention me by name, just as Hunter's assistant. But apparently I'm the devil incarnate, and of course the only people they spoke with were Simon and his friends. This Grafton guy smelled blood and went after it in a quasi-editorial way. So this is presented as his opinion and little more."

She tossed the pages onto the table and stomped out of the room. Monty closed his eyes and tried to will away the anger, resentment, and unfairness of it all. Jesus, Monty thought his family had issues, but Hunter's.... To do something like this to his own son, Simon had to have been having a temper tantrum.

His phone rang, and Monty checked that it wasn't some reporter or something, and answered it when he saw Hunter's number. "I saw the article, and I'll be right over."

"Just stay there," Hunter said. "I've been on the phone with everyone for the last hour. Garvin was angrier than I've ever seen him. He was on the phone with the Johnston people, and they aren't sure if they want to go ahead with the campaign or not. The publicists are working on damage control, but they all agreed that you and I shouldn't see each other. They want to let things calm down and see if everything will work out. They also said that I should meet with my dad, who apparently is contrite as hell, and get him to make a statement about what he said." Hunter sounded as though he'd been beaten halfway to hell.

Monty was stunned, but maybe he should have seen it coming. This whole thing was a real mess. "I guess we should have been more conscious of how things would look to other people." He sighed and was glad he was still sitting down.

"Yeah... well... things have a way of working out for a few weeks and then going all to crap." Monty knew exactly what Hunter was referring to. "I have to go. The coach is calling and I expect there's going to be hell to pay from him and team management." The line went dead, and Monty put his phone on the table, placed his head down, and let the tears, which had been threatening ever since he'd first read that damn thing, run down his cheeks.

"SWEETHEART, IT will be all right," his mother said that morning as Monty watched the local news. Apparently they were questioning the accuracy of the story already, but it seemed that the article had raised more questions, some of them in regard to Hunter's education and his color blindness. Neither the league nor the team had weighed in, so it was reporters asking questions and taking pictures from outside Hunter's house. "This whole thing will calm down. It's just the story of the day, and soon there will be something else to occupy their attention."

"Yeah, but this is going to cost Hunter so much. The deal he worked so hard for in New York could be history."

Monty knew this was going to work out, but at the moment, he didn't see how.

"You really care for him, don't you?" Monty almost pulled his hands back when she reached for them. "You know it's okay. I'm happy that you're happy."

"Thanks, Mom," Monty said. He was pleased she was happy for him, but he kept turning his attention to the television, hoping to hear some more about what was going on. Of course, every time the news came on, it was only a rehash of what they'd said before.

Camille switched to one of the sports stations, but they didn't seem to really care, as there were actual sports to broadcast. That was, until the break, only this time the commentator was questioning if Hunter's relationship with his assistant could be sexual harassment. Monty turned it off, and thankfully Em called them in to brunch.

"I know things look bad, but it will be okay," Camille said. "Stuff like this happens all the time. Believe me. And what happened isn't really all that bad."

"Of course not. If it was any other player, no one would care. He'd show up with a beautiful woman on his arm and say that she swept him off his feet and that they were madly in love, and every guy on earth would want to be him. But it's different. I'm another guy, and it doesn't matter if Hunter was already out of the closet." Monty moved to the kitchen and sat down at the table.

"I know. The league pretty much froze the last gay player out, and they could do that to Hunter," Camille said, sitting across from him. "But it isn't right."

"He said he's already been called in by the coach."

Camille nodded slowly. "I guess you're right. This whole thing is fixing to get ugly."

"Can we talk about something else?" Monty asked. There wasn't a dang thing he could do to help Hunter at this point. He'd talk to the press himself if he thought it would do any good, but he was afraid they'd twist whatever he said into something tawdry and ugly. No, it was best, as hard as it was going to be, to stay away and out of sight until this blew over.

"What about your job?"

"I guess I'll see what happens, but I suspect I'm going to need to get a new one. Even if this blows over, being Hunter's assistant probably isn't in the cards any longer." He should have known that all good things have to come to an end. Granted, his job was less important than Hunter. He could always get something else to pay the bills. Football was Hunter's life, and it looked like Monty may have had a hand in putting that in jeopardy.

"You can't give up so easily," Em said as she dished up eggs and bacon. Since Em had cooked, brunch was little more than breakfast by another name. Usually Monty would cook, but he didn't have the energy, and he appreciated that Emily had taken over for him.

"Hunter pointedly didn't say that he cared for me and that he was going to miss me or that he'd even call. He just said it would be best if we didn't see each other for a while. I don't need a bulldozer to hit me to understand."

"He's probably very busy and trying to contain the damage," Camille said, but Monty knew the real score. If Hunter had needed him, he'd be calling at least. It wasn't as though his phone was bugged, and Monty could try to help. Hunter had said he relied on him and cared for him but obviously not enough to stand by him.

"Whatever he's doing, I hope he's having some success and that he gets what he truly wants." Monty ate a few bites of egg and a slice of bacon before pushing his plate away. He didn't want to be a downer, so he excused himself and went to his room, closing the door behind him. Monty lay on his bed and put his phone on the nightstand. He willed himself to be wrong and for Hunter to call or text, anything to let him know he was all right. He kept telling himself Hunter was probably up to his ears in strategies and action plans to try to salvage his reputation, and he'd have to be patient.

"HEY, SLEEPYHEAD," Em said when Monty emerged from his room a few hours later. He had finally been able to rest, but his phone had remained silent.

"Anything?" he asked.

"No. Everything is quiet. Of course there won't be another paper until tomorrow, so there can't be anything on that front. The last story we saw was from in front of Hunter's house, but he didn't come out, and the police were moving everyone on because they couldn't block a residential street. I bet that pissed them off."

Monty smiled. "They won't give up as long as they smell scandal of any sort."

"True, but this isn't that juicy, and even the sports channel, where they brought up sexual harassment, hasn't said anything more on that topic. I think they realized they were skating on thin ice with that one."

"Has anyone mentioned my name?" Monty trudged into the living room.

"Not so far, but they have to be hunting around trying to find out who it is, and that story from New York isn't going to help, because if they follow that trail, they'll figure it out."

"So maybe I should leave for a while before the trail leads here and you have people parked outside trying to get a story." Monty went to the front window, expecting to see news trucks and God knew what else pulling up in front of the house, but the street was empty.

"Come on. Let's watch a movie and have a little fun to take our minds off this whole mess," Emily suggested. "Mom, can you pop some corn? I'll find a movie."

"Sure." She lifted herself off the sofa and went into the kitchen.

"I can do it."

"You sit down," his mother said, and Monty slumped on the sofa, checking his phone for the millionth time, it seemed like.

"Maybe I should text him," Monty said, and Emily flashed him a dirty look. "I know. It only makes me look needy."

"As you said, he was the one who told you to stay away, so do what he says and make him come back to you."

"What if he doesn't?" Monty asked.

"Then he doesn't deserve you, and there are so many other guys out there who would love to be with you. And once the word does leak out that you're Hunter's assistant, you'll have dozens of guys lining up to take you out."

"How do you figure that?" Monty asked as he scratched his head.

"Everyone is going to want to know how you captured Hunter Davis's interest and what makes you so special." Emily grinned, and Monty groaned.

"You're delusional. I'm not all that special. It's Hunter who was amazing. He was good to me, and he thought I was hot. And I know he liked me, which is why I don't understand this. I didn't do anything other than try to help him." But deep down he was afraid he knew exactly what was going on, and it chilled him to the core. Monty had heard much of the conversation between Hunter and his mother. He'd heard her warning about how Hunter would eventually have to choose, and when the time came, he'd hoped that Hunter would choose him over football, but he was afraid, with every passing hour, that he knew Hunter's choice.

The popcorn was ready, and Mom brought in a huge bowl. They all sat down, and Em put in *The Wedding Date*. Just what he needed—a romantic comedy. Still, Monty watched Debra Messing try to figure out where she'd screwed up her life. He always loved the dance lesson scene when she stomps on Dermot Mulroney's foot and he takes charge of the dance. Monty wished it was really that easy to get someone to see you and fall for you. Of course falling into love easily meant things could end just as quickly, as he was finding out. But he tried not to let the whole thing bother him. It had only been a day, for Christ's sake, and he was being as angsty as a twelve-year-old after his first kiss. Monty needed to back away and let things happen. It was the only way he was going to be able to see this through to the end. Whatever the hell it was.

"MONTY," HUNTER had said, and his pleading tone almost broke through Monty's hurt resolve. "The team, coaches, my publicist, they're all pressuring me to stay away and let this thing blow over. I… this is my career and I… they've backed me into a corner and…." Hunter's voice faltered.

Monty collapsed back onto the sofa at home, closing his eyes. "Playing football has to come first after all." He hoped he sounded at least a little snide, but it hurt, regardless of Hunter's explanation, that he was choosing his career over him. Monty should have known, if push came to shove, he was the one who would lose, but it still hurt.

"I have to go, but I did want to try to explain. I hope—" Hunter cut himself off and quickly said good-bye before ending the call.

That had been a few days ago, and Monty had heard nothing since.

Just as Camille predicted, things had quieted down—until Monday evening when Hunter and his father made a joint statement alongside the coach and even the team manager.

"Yes, I am a gay football player, but I have not given up my right to a personal life. I know there are fans out there who will find this difficult to understand, but I am not going to change the person that I am." Monty leaned closer to the television. "At some time in the future I might be in a relationship with another person, and that should not be a shock to anyone. If I were straight, my relationships would not be of much interest to anyone. I do my best for the Philadelphia Red Hawks, and I always will. But in return I ask for respect and the privacy to conduct my life." Hunter looked amazing in a pair of pants and shirt that Monty helped him buy. Hunter turned to his father, who took the microphone.

"I have learned a number of things in the past few days. My son is stronger than I ever gave him credit for, and as a father I am exceedingly proud of him. I haven't always respected his independence. He's my son and I see him as the child I raised. But Hunter is an adult, and he deserves the same respect and dignity as any other person, regardless of their profession or sexual orientation." Monty was pretty sure that someone else had written that statement for Simon.

Once he was done, Simon moved to stand next to Hunter's mother, and the coach of the Red Hawks took the microphone. "Each and every one of our players will be treated with the same human dignity, and we will stand behind all our players just as we stand behind Hunter. He is an asset to the organization and a key member of the team. The fact that he is gay is irrelevant to us." The coach grew silent and stared straight at the camera. "We will take a few questions."

"Hunter, what about your assistant? There have been allegations of sexual harassment. Are those true?" a reporter asked.

Hunter smiled his winning smile, and Monty's heart leapt for a few seconds. "Those so-called allegations were fabricated in the news media. I did have a relationship with my assistant. He is an amazing man, and I was lucky enough to have had him in my life." Monty thought Hunter was speaking right to him, and damn it all, if with every word, Monty didn't know he was coming closer and closer to the end and to a broken heart. "Our relationship was consensual, and I care for him very much."

Hunter pointed to someone else.

"What about the revelations that you're color-blind. Are those true?"

"Yes. I was born that way, and I have spent much of my life working to overcome the challenges that has put in my way. I do want to stress that color blindness is a natural and normal situation for me. I don't see any differently today than I did three days ago, and it certainly doesn't affect my ability to play. It does mean that under certain situations, I have to work harder, but I've lived with that for twenty-three years."

"We see no reason why this should affect Hunter's ability to play quality football," the coach added, to put an end to that line of questioning.

Monty couldn't watch any longer and switched the station. He did pick up his phone and send Hunter a message.

I saw your press conference. He typed a bunch more about assuming that Hunter didn't want him as his assistant any longer and that he'd send the equipment he had back to Helen at his agent's office, but he deleted all of it. *You sounded really good.* He sent the message and waited for a response. But one didn't come through. He thought of sending an "I miss you" text, but didn't. It had been nearly three days since he'd heard a single word from Hunter, and he'd been able to get the message loud and clear.

He packed up the equipment that he'd been sent, including the phone he'd been using, and when he was out, made a special trip downtown to Garvin's office. He arrived just before five and hoped he'd catch Helen before she left for the day. He supposed, if he had to, he could leave the stuff with the receptionist for her… or with security or something.

When he arrived, he asked for Helen, and the receptionist told him to have a seat while she called her. Helen came out with a slight scowl on her face.

"I wanted to bring back the equipment you sent."

Helen took what Monty gave her, and he turned to get the hell out of here as fast as he could, but she said, "Monty."

"Yeah, sorry."

Helen looked around. "Come with me," she said and led him into a small conference room just off the agency's lobby. "Did he fire you?"

"He hasn't said a word to me in three days. Not a text, e-mail, or phone call. I saw the press conference today and figured from what he'd said that I may as well turn everything in and find another job." He wasn't going to get maudlin or act like some heartbroken teenager. He was going to be fine.

Helen didn't look happy, and Monty got the feeling there were things she wanted to tell him but couldn't. Not that it mattered all that damn much.

"Thank you for everything," Monty said and left the room, hurrying back out to his car before the lump in his throat got so big he couldn't breathe.

THAT EVENING he got a call from a number he didn't recognize. Monty almost didn't answer it but took a chance, fully expecting to hang up.

"Monty, it's Joe Clark."

"Hi, Joe," Monty said.

"I don't know how to say this, but I sort of figured that with the whole brouhaha around Hunter that… well, I don't know what's going to happen, but if you need a job, I could use someone to help organize things for me, and I bet Mark could as well. So can other members of the team. You could probably help a lot of us." Joe paused, and Monty felt his unease growing a little. "I don't get the being gay thing, but I don't suppose I have to in order to know that you're a good guy and can really help us keep things organized. Hell, I suspect Mark would hire you just for the cookies."

Monty was overwhelmed. "Thanks, Joe. I appreciate the offer. I really do."

"Things like this happen from time to time, and no one is blaming you for any of it. Sometimes what we do is all about perceptions. Like I said, I don't understand you being gay, but I'm smart enough to know that Hunter isn't the only gay player. He's just the only one we know about, and I think that's sad." He seemed to be settling into a theme. "When he first joined the team, I avoided Hunter at all costs because I thought I'd get… I don't know."

"Painted with the same gay brush?" Monty supplied.

"I think so. But Hunter is a great guy, and I came to see that. My mother passed away during the season, and it was really hard. We had to schedule the funeral around games, and Hunter was there the whole time like a huge watchdog to make sure we had some private time. He's a great person, and that's all that matters." The nerves returned to Joe's voice. "I guess I'm jittery, but I wanted you to know that you have a job if you want it."

Monty wasn't sure if this was some sort of inclusivity exercise for Joe, but he appreciated him taking the time and making the effort. "Thank you for that. Like you said, I don't know what's going to happen."

"If you need a job, call me, and we'll work something out. But for the record," Joe said, and Monty tensed, "I was in the room with you two, and dang, the way you were acting with each other, that I do get, because you acted just like Sue did when we first got together. Wait, that didn't come out right. I didn't mean to say that you were a girl, or—"

"It's all right, Joe. I understand what you're saying," Monty said with a little amusement.

"I meant that you looked happy, and so did Hunter."

"I know. Thank you." Monty smiled even though Joe couldn't see it. "I appreciate the job offer and what you said. It takes a strong person to change their mind sometimes." Monty wasn't sure what else to say, and thankfully Joe said good-bye and ended the call.

"Who was that?" Em asked as she came in the room, yawning and ready for bed in her unicorn pajamas.

"One of the players. He said that if things go south as far as my job with Hunter, that he'd like me to help get him organized, and that some of the other players might as well. I thought it was really nice of him."

"Monty, you are so talented. Maybe you should talk to this agent of Hunter's and see if he has a job for you. You'd be really good at it."

"Yeah, like Garvin is going to hire me after all this mess that he had to help clean up." Monty hugged her. "It's not a bad idea, though, and maybe once things quiet down, I can talk to Helen and see what she thinks." He really liked her and was going to miss talking to her. "It's time for me to go to bed. I've spent enough time today feeling sorry for myself. I messaged Hunter today and he isn't answering me, so tomorrow I'll have to pick up the pieces and figure out what I'm going to do."

"It'll work out." Em hugged him and went to her and Camille's room, closing the door. Monty turned off the television and the lights, made sure the front door was locked, and went to bed.

CHAPTER 11

"ARE THEY serious about this?" Hunter asked, jumping to his feet in front of Garvin's desk. "They knew I was gay when we signed the contract, and now they're saying that... what the fuck?" He was so angry he could barely think straight. "They want me to lead some sort of celibate life. Is that in the contract?"

"No. But they can decide not to use the images and cancel the campaign," Garvin said, trying to be conciliatory.

"But they still have to pay me," Hunter said with a smile, and he knew he was right. "Look." He tapped the top of the desk. "It's your job to get them to see things right. I am who I am, and they knew it before anything happened. And you tell them that this whole thing is much ado about nothing. The league is happy, and I'm looking like a victim rather than a guy who did something wrong."

"You know what the team manager said. They have reservations because you being gay makes you vulnerable to this kind of thing."

"Who the hell cares? The league welcomed back a guy who had been convicted and spent time in prison for dog fighting, but they're squeamish about the gay thing? It's your job to be in my corner on this one, and I don't feel as though you have been. I've done the stupid press conference the way you wanted, and dammit...." He'd seen the text that Monty had sent him and Hunter had cringed. That was exactly what he'd been afraid of. It damn near broke his heart to say those words, but the team, his agent, and even his publicist had said it was what he had to do. "You need to fix this. I won't have my life held hostage."

"They can back out of the contract."

"But not for a good reason and not based on lies and someone's opinion. There was no proof of anything, and in the end I'm more

155

popular than ever. The sports shows are saying that I'm being held to a different standard. Did you watch ESPN this morning?"

"I did, and that's great news, but it's too soon to tell if that's going to be the lasting reaction, and Johnston is nervous right now. It's just bad timing."

"Then get them unnervous and tell them to man up. I'll do my part in the agreement, and you remind them that it isn't only women who buy underwear for their husbands. Gay men buy it too—look at brands marketed directly to them." Hunter was angry and getting more so by the minute. "I listened to all of you, and in the end I'm the one who's getting sold up the river." He leaned over the desk, eyes wide, staring at Garvin. "You fucking work for me. Never forget that. So do your damn job and look out for my best interests, or I will find someone else who will. Do you understand?" Hunter turned and left the office. He'd had enough of all this.

Helen was at her desk outside, and Hunter stopped to briefly say hello and try to let the frustration that had taken over flow away. "I'm sorry you had to hear that."

She rolled her eyes and glanced into Garvin's office. "You give him hell when you need to. It's good for him."

"What did you say?" Garvin asked from his desk.

"I said you were being an ass," Helen retorted, and Hunter stifled a grin. She turned to him. "Monty was here yesterday, and he dropped off his computer and things."

"How did he look?" Hunter asked the first thing that came into his mind.

"Angry as hell and miserable."

"Did he say anything?"

"I tried to give him a place where he could talk, but Monty handed me the computer and phone and raced out of there. It doesn't take a genius to know that he's hurting."

Shit. The last of Hunter's anger ebbed away, replaced by the loneliness that washed over him whenever he was alone. "I don't know what to do."

Helen shook her head. "You're a football player. On the gridiron you battle and fight to win. Why should this be any different? The season hasn't even started, and all this is a bunch of bullshit, because what matters is what happens on the field. The rest is distraction."

"Helen, you should be my agent instead of him," Hunter said loudly enough for Garvin to hear.

"Bastard," Garvin said, and when Hunter leaned in to look into his office, he flipped him off while returning to his phone conversation, which sounded a lot like the one Hunter had just had with him. Hunter turned back to Helen, who seemed to be debating something.

"Life is all about choices. And I see plenty of players come through here. They are up one minute and down the next. Sometimes it's because they weren't good enough, and other times it's because of the choices they made. You are at a point where you need to make hard decisions, and you can't have it all, no one can."

"I know. My mom had a talk with me a while ago. I just wish I knew what to do."

Helen pulled open her desk drawer and pulled out a framed photograph. "I never show this to anyone. This is my Kenny. He was your age when this was taken. That was ten years ago. He was in a car accident and ended up on life support. The doctors said there was no hope, but my husband wasn't about to give up. Kenny lingered on machines for months, and I couldn't decide what to do. John eventually said he'd abide by whatever I wanted. I knew it was a cop-out on his part in a way, but I had to make the decision to turn off the machines and let him go." Helen reached into her desk drawer to get a tissue, and Hunter took one as well. "I had to make the decision to end my son's life, and there are days I wish I still had him. I wish the accident had never happened, but I did what my heart told me to do. I had to let him go. It was time. And while I have regrets in my life, I don't regret that because I made that decision out of love and with love. So you figure out what's really important to you and listen to your heart. Business deals come and go, and endorsements will happen as long as you play well." Helen blew her nose. "Sorry, when I get maudlin, I start to spout clichés, but you get what I'm trying to say." She wiped her eyes and put the picture back in the drawer.

"Why don't you keep it on your desk?"

"Because Kenny is always with me, and I like having him near, but it's still difficult for me to talk about. So I keep Kenny close and private." She closed the drawer and shifted her gaze to his. "I'd be proud to have you as my son, and if you were my son, I'd tell you that the most important thing in life is to find someone to love and who loves you. That will last beyond a football career, longer than some promotional campaign, and can be the one thing that you can carry with you through the rest of your life."

"Helen," Garvin called, and she rolled her eyes before standing to get back to work.

"Thank you," Hunter said, and she patted his chest lightly before joining Garvin in his office and closing the door. Hunter left the agency and went home.

EMILY WAS waiting for him with fire in her eyes. "We had an appointment," she said.

"I didn't think you'd come after... well...." Hunter unlocked the door and let her inside, grateful the press was gone from outside the house. "What can I do for you?" He picked up the books from the coffee table and handed them to her. "I did read them, and I really do appreciate what you tried to do for me." He shifted his weight from foot to foot because, hell, he was nervous as shit. Emily looked about ready to rip his balls off.

"What the hell are you playing at?" Emily asked, starting a barrage of words that flew at him fast and furious. "Were you just playing with Monty? Because if you were, your nuts are so in jeopardy. He's been sitting at home wondering if you're okay. Do you get that?" She stepped closer, and Hunter took a step back. This woman could intimidate the biggest guy on the field. "You treated him like shit, and he's still worried about you." She took a breath, and Hunter wondered if he could get a word in. "Hell, he feels guilty, for some reason, over what happened, and it isn't his fault. So shit happens, big deal. It happens to everybody, and it isn't the end of the world."

"Monty was worried about me?"

"Of course he was. Monty has, like, the biggest heart of anyone I know, and you stomped all over it. He fell in love with you, ya idiot, and so help me, I want to kick your gay ass into the middle of next week."

"Is that why you came here, to threaten me?"

"Hell, no. That's just a side benefit. I came to get my books back and to tell you to pull your head out of your ass." She turned, yanking open the front door. Hunter blinked in surprise, and she was gone, in her car, racing out of the drive.

It seemed that no matter what he did, he couldn't get it right. Hunter flopped down on the sofa and punched the cushions repeatedly. He was so damn frustrated, because he knew what he wanted, and to top it off, his mother had been right. He couldn't have everything, and he was going to have to choose.

"DUDE," CLYDE said as they sat around the poker table the following evening at Joe's house. "Where are the goodies from Monty?"

"Where've you been?" Mark asked quickly. "That whole mess with Hunter circled around Monty, and the coach and team told him he had to put distance between him and Monty. I mean, we can do what we want, but the hint of some kind of hanky-panky on Hunter's part and they're all squicky."

"I talked to Monty yesterday and told him that, if he needed a job, I could use his help," Joe said, flooring Hunter. Joe was the last guy he would have expected to build those kinds of bridges. "He's a good guy, and he got you straightened out. Hell, anyone who can get you places on time has to be some kind of magician."

"You offered Monty a job?" Hunter asked.

"Hell yeah, I did. The guy is awesomely organized, and it seems that you don't need him anymore. Though you did show up late tonight, so you sure as hell need something. Because, man, if you go back to being the guy who can't get anywhere on time, I may have to kick your ass. It's no fun waiting around for you all the damn time."

Hunter couldn't get over the fact that Monty was getting job offers from other players, even though he hadn't actually fired him or anything. In fact, Hunter had requested that his accountant continue to pay him, because he didn't want to hurt Monty. "This whole thing is out of control."

"And whose fault is that?" Clyde asked. "I raise you all ten." He tossed in the chips. "Are we going to play or just talk about Hunter's fucked-up love life?" He set his cards facedown on the table. "That's what all this is. Everyone is telling you what to do and who to see... and all that shit. The crappy thing is that you're listening to those assholes. You're the playmaker, the guy the team looks to for inspiration and stuff. Mostly it's older guys who do that, but for us, it's you." The other men around the table nodded.

"You're there for everyone. You listen to all their bullshit and let them get it out. But in this case, you gotta listen to you and what you want." Mark threw in his chips, and Hunter folded.

"So I should tell coach and the team to screw off?"

"No. But they overstepped and they know it. You did nothing wrong except find someone you liked. If Monty happens to be a little close to home, change that and get him a new job, but keep Monty. That guy is so worth it," Clyde said.

Hunter was having a hard time processing all this. Sure, these were his friends, but he didn't expect this kind of support from them. He was the gay one after all, and he'd figured they'd want some distance when he had trouble. "But it goes further than the team."

"It always does." Clyde was normally quiet. He played well, was a good guy, and didn't say much. But this seemed to have touched a nerve, because he talked more tonight than Hunter could ever remember before. "See, once I was the hotshot guy like you. I was new and good-looking and they wanted me to do commercials, but I can't. The thought of talking to people and reporters like this terrifies me, and I'd clam up."

"You stare down the offensive line for a living," Joe said.

"Yeah, but they aren't microphone-shaped. Anyway, I tried to do it and managed to make it work because my agent and my mom and dad wanted me to. But I hated it, and a few years ago I said I wasn't going to do it no more. The money wasn't worth it. I play and I'm good at it, but that's enough. It's all I want." He turned to Hunter. "You got to decide what it is that you want. Screw the rest of the shit and go back to the core. If you want to let the team and everybody else say who you can have in your life so you can play football, or if you want to sell underwear, potato chips, or adult diapers, then that's what you do."

"Thanks, Clyde." He patted him on the shoulder, and they finished playing the hand, which Clyde won.

"I'll also let the rest of you know. No matter what, this is my last season playing. Me and my wife have talked it over, and I don't know what I'm gonna do, but this is it. I ain't gonna play until I'm too old and get hit too many times and turn my brain to mush." He grew quiet again, and play resumed.

HUNTER WENT home after the game, keyed up as all hell. Everyone was telling him the same thing, and he hadn't wanted to hear it, because… well, because he thought he knew better than everyone else and because he was a fool. Hunter paced the house for a while, too excited to sleep, and thought about texting Monty, but he had no right to, regardless of how much he missed him. Hunter had lost that right, and he deserved to be alone and miserable. He ended up watching movies until all hours, falling asleep alone on the sofa.

He woke to banging on the front door. Bleary and rumpled, he pulled it open to find his dad standing on his steps. "What do you want?" He was too blinky to be nice. He and his dad had done their thing in front of the cameras, but that didn't mean they had worked things out. It was more like his mother had threatened his father with divorce and castration if he didn't do it.

"What have you been doing, son?" he asked, looking him over.

"I fell asleep on the couch. Look, I have a bunch of things to do."

"I'm sure showering and changing clothes are high on that list," his dad said, stepping past him and into the house.

Hunter groaned. He wasn't in the mood for this. "Why are you here?"

"Because of this whole bullshit mess between us," he said. "We've been a team since you were a kid, and now we've got nothing."

"Dad, we stopped being a team a long time ago. I went on to do the things you always wanted for me, and you became a hanger-on." Hunter scratched his head and led the way into the living room. "You were just using me to get in with your friends."

"I may have gotten carried away."

Hunter knew it was hard for his dad to admit that. "Dad, you were using my house and my things like they were your own. That wasn't fair or right. All you had to do was ask, but you never did. You assumed and then you took." Hunter sat down. "And what's worse, you blamed my assistant for it and then aired your grievances in front of a reporter. You didn't even have the guts to come here and talk to me about it."

"I'm your father, and you should have come talk to me."

"I wasn't the one in the wrong. I could have been nicer about it, but you never listened, so I was harsh with you, I admit that, but that's as far as I'm going to go." Hunter stared him down as though he were an angry defenseman. He wasn't going to give a single inch and let his dad get the better of him. "I'm going to be the one in charge of my own life and my own things. I'm not going to let you or anyone make my decisions for me."

His father lowered his gaze. "I'm happy to hear that, son. Is Monty here right now?"

"No. The league and team have been pressuring me to keep some distance from him until this blows over."

"That doesn't sound to me like what you said you were going to do."

"It isn't. Dad, I did what they wanted, and apparently Monty thinks I've fired him and don't want him around... but I do. It's my fault, and I handled this all wrong." Hunter stood back up and went into the kitchen with his dad following. "He used to make me breakfast. Nothing fancy, but he knew what I liked. Hell, Dad, when he came for his interview, he brought me coffee because he thought I might want a cup." Hunter thought about all the times Monty had been there with little things that he never asked for but were just there because he thought Hunter would want them. "I keep thinking about Michael, Dad."

"The boy who killed himself when you were in college?"

"Yeah. I always thought I failed him, and now I think I did the same thing to Monty." Hunter poured a glass of juice for himself and his dad.

"Then I have one thing to say. What are you going to do to get him back?" His dad took the glass, and Hunter clinked with him before drinking his down.

That is a good question.

HIS FATHER stayed with Hunter for a while, and they talked through many of their issues, allowing Hunter to air his grievances. It came down to respect, and Hunter wasn't going to back down from that.

"So what are you going to do?" his father asked after an hour.

"I don't know."

"You hurt this young man, you realize that? I did my part by bringing on this situation, but in the end you hurt him."

Hunter acknowledged his actions with a single nod. "You had to have messed things up with Mom at one point."

"Yeah."

"What did you do?" Hunter asked.

"I bought her the biggest ring I could afford, got down on one knee, and asked her to marry me in the best restaurant I couldn't afford. And it was so worth it." Hunter had never seen his father look mushy before.

"I don't think that's going to work for me."

"Probably not. But why don't you start by telling him how you feel. Or better yet, show him how you feel. I'm not a guy who usually spends a lot of time on romantic gestures. Your mother knows that, and she understands. But when it matters, I do bring her flowers so she knows it's a big deal. She also knows I love her, and I show her in my own way."

"That's really helpful, Dad."

"Your mother once told me that everyone has their own way of showing love. Hers is cooking and all that gardening she does."

"Huh...," Hunter said.

"Your mother gardened all those years so I would come home to a house that was bright, colorful, and welcoming. And she cooked because she knew I loved to eat. It took me a long time before I realized that. I dare say your Monty does some of what he does because he cares about you. Like he helped find someone so you can read better. He didn't do that for himself. Monty did that for you. So whatever you do, make sure it's something that comes from your heart, and then Monty will know exactly how you feel."

"All right." He was thinking that jewelry or a nice gift would work, but from what his dad said, there had to be more to it. Monty was a good person, and he hadn't known quite how to react when Hunter gave him things because he hadn't been interested in what Hunter had. Monty had been interested in him.

His dad left, and Hunter sat on his sofa, trying to figure out what in the hell he wanted to do.

CHAPTER 12

"MONTY, YOUR phone is ringing," Emily said from the other end of the sofa. She answered it and then handed it to him. "It's a guy named Joe."

"Hey," Monty said as cheerfully as he could, but he really wasn't feeling it.

"I was wondering if you could help me out. I have a mess with schedules and receipts and things like that. Hunter had said that you were able to fix it for him. So could you help me out? My wife is giving me so much damn grief because I can't seem to get where I'm supposed to be when I have to pick up the kids. Their schedule is more complex than any running play ever devised."

"Okay. I can try," Monty said. "When do you want me to come over and take a look?"

"How about tonight? If I don't get a handle on this, I'm a dead man."

"Okay. Give me the address, and I'll be there in an hour or so." It wasn't like he had anything better to do on a Thursday night.

"Awesome. I'll text it over." Joe sounded so happy and relieved. "See you soon." He hung up, and Monty did the same.

"Em, I have to go. I'm going to be helping Joe Clark."

"Not *the* Joe Clark?" Camille asked, poking her head out of the kitchen. "Shit, you're the gay one and have no idea about these guys, yet you have them calling you for help and shit. How do you rate?" Camille stuck her tongue out.

"I'm cute. That opens doors everywhere." He grabbed his bag, as his phone pinged, and he left the apartment and headed toward Joe's, using the phone's GPS to guide him. During the drive, he kept telling himself he was doing this because he needed the money, but he knew he was really hoping to hear something, anything, about Hunter. Monty was totally screwed and he needed to get over him.

Monty pulled up in front of Joe's house. It was nothing like what he expected. Joe lived in a large, twenties-era stone home that took his breath away. It was one of the old Main Line mansions that Monty had always wanted to be able to look inside of. He'd been expecting something new and plastic feeling, rather than a home with a grace that could only be born of age and solidity. The yard was manicured and perfect with plenty of spring color to catch the eye. It was clear that Joe and his wife loved their home very much.

The front door opened as he approached, and two boys hurried out.

"Are you Mr. Monty?" the oldest one said. "Daddy told me to bring you around this way." He smiled with missing front teeth and led Monty along a stepping-stone path, around the side of the house, and through a gate that he had to stand on his tiptoes to open. The other boy walked alongside Monty, looking up at him every few steps.

"We're back here," Joe called and met them at the gate. He lifted the youngest into his arms. "Thank you for getting him."

He smiled and hugged his dad, resting his head on Joe's shoulder. "This is Petey, and that's David," Joe said. "Sue made some dinner, and I thought we could sit down to eat, and then we can go over everything." Joe led the way to a table under a stunning pergola that was covered with blooming lavender-colored wisteria.

There was no one else there.

"What's going on?" Monty said.

"Well, there's a friend of mine who wanted to see you, and he asked for our help," Joe said as he took David's hand. "Mommy has dinner almost ready." Joe headed to the sliding glass doors and the boys hurried inside, and then Hunter stepped outside.

Monty stared at him, and Hunter looked down at himself, blushing. "Sue picked this out for me." He came over and handed Monty a huge bouquet of roses.

166

"You look nice, but what's all this about?" Monty asked. "You could have called me in the last week and let me know you were alive, that you didn't hate me, or told me what the hell was going on with my job." Monty wasn't letting Hunter off because of some flowers and a hangdog look. "Now you hand me these and stand there looking hot as all get-out, and I'm supposed to just forgive you and everything will go back to the way it was? Well, you have a lot to learn."

"Yes, I do," Hunter said. "I really do. But that's not what I'm doing. Well, I did give you flowers and I do look hot, at least Sue said I did, though Joe thinks I'm a thickheaded pain in the ass, and they're both probably right. But I did this because I wanted to show you something."

"But why have me come here?" Monty clutched the two-dozen roses in his hands.

"Because I can't cook for crap and I didn't want to take you out for dinner. Sue agreed to help me out. See, my mom told me that someday I'd have to make a choice."

"Yeah. Between football and me, and I know what you chose. It was clear as hell when you were on television." Monty wanted to slap his hand over his mouth. He'd forgotten for a second that he'd overheard that. "Sorry. You weren't being quiet. Anyway, now that you've made your choice, you want to try to smooth things over so you can have everything."

Hunter shook his head. "No." He moved nearer. "I was told by the team and the league that I should stop seeing you so that the whole gay thing would calm down. It was fine if I was gay as long as I was a good, quiet little gay boy and didn't do anything like have a life."

Monty shoved the flowers back at Hunter. "So these are to get me to go along and be some sort of boyfriend on the sly?" He was so angry.

"No!" Hunter snapped, and he pushed the flowers back to him. "These are because I choose you. Pure and simple. Joe told me the same thing my mom did, and I have to make a choice, so I choose you. I'll live my life in the open, with you. You'll have to quit working for me, but Joe, Mark, and Clyde want to hire you to help them. We all have schedules that are complicated, and you did an amazing job for me, so they want your help."

"So you've decided everything?"

"No. I haven't. I talked to my dad, and he said that he once did something really stupid when he was dating my mom, and when I asked him how he made it up to her, he said he asked her to marry him."

Monty set the flowers on the table and glared at him. "If you think—"

"I'm not going to ask you to marry me. Not now," Hunter said. "But I do want you to know how I feel about you." Hunter held up his hand and removed the ring he wore. "This is my team ring. The guys got together at the end of the year and had it made for me." Hunter showed it to him. It was gold and it had the team mascot on the top. It read "Red Hawks Playmaker" around the edge. Hunter took his hand and slipped the ring on it. "I want you to have it."

"But...."

"Monty, you're my playmaker. When I need something, you're there, even if I don't know I need it. You see something wrong and you fix it. If I need help, you find someone to do it, and you always make me feel better about myself." A tear rolled down Hunter's cheek, and Monty wiped away his own. "I love you, Monty. I have since that day in New York."

"When we were playing football?" Monty asked, and Hunter shook his head.

"Football is so not your thing. But I love that you tried." Hunter wiped his eyes. "It was watching you at the boat pond. You were so delighted, and I remember thinking that I wanted to make you look like that all the time. And I will if you'll let me."

"Hunter." Monty wasn't ready to let himself give in. "What about your endorsements and things?"

"Garvin grew a set of balls and went at them. It seems that the campaign is not only going ahead but is being moved up to take advantage of my notoriety."

"So everything worked out?" Monty asked.

"No. There was another deal Garvin was working on and they backed out. I'm sure there will be others too, but that doesn't matter. I made a decision to live my life openly and with you, the man I love. The rest will fall into line." Hunter took the final step forward to stand toe-to-toe with him.

"You hurt me, Hunter." Monty steeled his gaze. "I've spent days with a hole in my heart that you put there. In one fell swoop I lost you, my job, and then you...." Monty smacked Hunter on the chest.

"I know. I did what they wanted and only hurt you more." Hunter lowered his gaze.

"What really hurt was that you chose them over me. Do you know how that feels?" Monty blinked to try to get his eyes dry and clear, but it wasn't really working too well.

"I think I do now." Hunter lowered his gaze. "I was a fool. I should have stood up to them and told them all to take a flying leap. I was happy, and you made me that way, and I... I should have been strong like you."

"I'm not strong." Monty wondered where Hunter was going with this.

"Yes, you are. You're one of the strongest people I know. You put up with me and stand up for yourself. You even stood up for me, and I couldn't return the favor when the time came." Hunter's voice broke, and Monty felt his resolve crumbling. "I should have told them all to go to hell. That you were more important than football."

"Am I?" Monty had to ask. That was the heart of the issue, and he had to know.

"Yes. Football is a game and you... you're my life." Hunter's sincerity rang like a bell and broke down the last of Monty's resolve.

Monty's breath hitched as he heard the words he hadn't expected he'd ever hear. "Hunter." The name came out as a whisper.

"Will you have me?"

Monty blinked. "Will I have you?" Fuck, tears welled in his eyes again and he blinked them away. "Of course I will. I love you

169

too. But if you do anything like this ever again, I'll smack you into the middle of next week. I swear to God." Hunter hugged him, and Monty closed his eyes, going willingly into his arms.

"I won't. I felt like crap the whole time."

"Don't you dare say you thought you'd get over me or some such bull-pucky," Monty said, "or I'll slap you here and now." Lord knows Monty had tried, but his thoughts had always gone back to Hunter.

"It was more like I thought I'd learn to live without you telling me what to do and pushing me to better myself." Hunter tightened his hug. "I guess I have a thing for pushy cute guys."

"As long as you know what your kink is, I can live with that." He held Hunter in return and heard soft giggles as a door slid open. Monty turned toward the house, realizing they had an audience. He didn't want to make anyone uncomfortable, but Hunter held him right where he was.

"I'll put these flowers in some water, and then we can have dinner," said a woman who Monty assumed was Joe's wife, Sue, as she set a dish on the table, then hurried back inside with the flowers. "Why don't you bring me these every once in a while?" The door slid closed, and Hunter groaned.

"Joe is going to kill me," Hunter said softly.

"I like it here. This is nice."

"You always spread warmth and cook, and Sue is the best cook I know, other than you, but don't tell her or there will be hell to pay."

"Got it."

"Besides, Joe was the one who finally managed to get the message through my thick head. He said that he'd made the same kind of decision a while ago and that he wouldn't change it." Hunter kissed the top of Monty's head. "God, I missed you. Even the way you smell...."

"Tell me about it." Monty buried his nose against Hunter's skin. He wished to hell they were someplace private so he could strip Hunter down and get an even better whiff of the man, as well as other things he didn't dare think about with children potentially watching.

"What did Joe say?" Monty asked, getting his mind out of the gutter.

"That I was a fool."

"I said that football was temporary and that love lasts forever." Joe brought out a platter of meat, and Sue followed with more food. Hunter broke the embrace, and they all went to the table. The dinner arrangement wasn't what Monty would have thought of as a particularly romantic setting, but seeing Joe and Sue together, watching each other across the table and then looking at their sons, proved there was love here, plenty of it. And when Monty caught Hunter's gaze, the warmth of the evening was magnified by ten.

"See, I told you," Joe said.

"What?" Monty asked, following Joe's gaze to Sue.

"You look at each other the way Joe used to look at me."

"Used to?" Joe asked with a raise of his eyebrows.

"How did you used to look at Mommy?" David asked, and Joe made a face that sent both boys into giggling fits.

"Now eat your dinner," Joe reminded them, and they returned to their plates. Both boys seemed to have their father's appetite.

"Are you going to play football like your dad?" Monty asked, but both boys shook their heads.

"I'n goona be a fireman," Petey said with his mouth half-full.

"I wanna be a violinist. I can show you later," David pronounced without setting his fork down.

"Joe and I decided that if the boys want to be active in sports, that we'd support them but not push it."

"David is quite the musician," Joe said, as proud as anything.

Monty leaned closer to Hunter. At the moment he couldn't think of anywhere he'd rather be.

EPILOGUE

"OH GOD!" Monty cried as Hunter leaned over him, teasing Monty's opening with his cock. "Don't tease me."

"Sweetheart, I'm just drawing out the excitement," Hunter said, and Monty tugged him down into a kiss and then pushed him away.

"Don't pull that sweetheart crap—just fuck me," Monty growled. Hunter pushed forward, and his cock breached Monty for the very first time unsheathed. Damn it all to hell, what a difference that made. Hunter and only Hunter sliding inside him.

"Jesus," Hunter moaned as he sank deeper.

"Yeah, that's it. Now give it to me and let me feel it while I'm watching you this afternoon. My own personal football player." Monty grabbed Hunter's legs and pulled him closer and deeper. Every time he'd woken during the night, he'd thought about riding Hunter halfway to hell, but today was the first game, so Hunter needed his sleep.

Hunter withdrew, pressed his cock to Monty's entrance again, and stilled. "And you're my own personal playmaker." Hunter slid in hard and deep, taking Monty's breath away. "Now hang on, baby, because this is going to be fast." Hunter snapped his hips, charging forward, taking what he wanted and giving Monty the ride of his life, sending him into orbit until they both reached the peak and floated back into each other's arms.

Hunter held him, and Monty drifted off to sleep, happy and sated… for now.

IT ALWAYS shocked him that after making love, all Hunter had to do was look at him with heat and he was ready for more.

"What time do you have to be at the stadium?" Monty asked.

"By noon. The game starts at two."

"Okay." Monty reached for his phone, but Hunter stopped him.

"It's seven in the morning. You can send the guys their reminder messages in a few hours. They need their sleep." Six team members employed Monty to coordinate their schedules and help keep their professional lives organized. He loved the work, and all of the guys were amazing in their own ways.

"I know. But it's the first game of the season, and I want everything to be awesome." Monty smiled, and his gaze shifted to the picture on the wall across from the bed. It was Hunter's near-naked underwear ad. They had chosen a bikini-briefs photo. Hunter leapt out of the image with enough heat to scorch the carpet.

"I still don't understand why you had to hang that in here." Hunter must have followed his gaze.

"That's easy. I can't stand in the middle of Times Square, where you're fifty feet tall, and jack off. So I hung it in here, and when you're not around, I use it for inspiration." Monty tried to stifle a nervous giggle, but Hunter grabbed him around the waist and tugged him right against him.

"You're a goof, and when we go on the road, you're going with us. The guys will need you to help keep them organized, and Lord knows I need you." Hunter sucked lightly on his neck. "But you are not taking that picture with you."

"That's okay. I had a wallet size made."

"You goof," Hunter said again, laughing. "Can we be serious for a minute?"

"Okay," Monty said, wondering what was up.

"You spend most of your time here, and with Camille announcing her pregnancy, don't you think it's time you moved in with me full-time?" Hunter stroked lightly down his arm.

"Okay," Monty answered.

Hunter stopped, blinking at him. "That's it?"

"Of course. All you had to do was ask," Monty said. "I've been waiting." Sometimes the man was slow on the uptake when it came to things like that, but he'd been busy with practices and games, so

Monty gave him a break. He let Hunter chew on that and closed his eyes once again. He was warm, comfortable, and happy as all hell. There was nothing he wanted more at the moment.

"Do you want kids?" Hunter asked, and Monty shot out of bed like he was on fire. Children were something they hadn't talked about.

"Where did that come from? I'll be Uncle Monty to my sister's child and the kids of any of your player friends, but you're the biggest kid I know, so that's more than enough." Monty leaned over the bed, kissed Hunter, and then headed for the bathroom. "Don't scare me like that." Monty grew serious. "Do you want kids?"

"My mom would love grandchildren," Hunter said quietly, and Monty returned to the bed and climbed back under the covers.

"Doesn't matter. Do *you* want children? I'm willing to consider it if that's what you really want, but we aren't going to have children to produce grandchildren for your parents." Monty leaned closer. "That isn't something I really ever considered."

"We don't have to decide now."

"No. But do you want them?" Monty pressed.

Hunter shrugged. "I don't know."

"Then let's not worry about that and just get you through the season." Monty pushed back the covers, climbed out, and raced for the bathroom. He used the facilities and got cleaned up. Then he dressed and went to the kitchen.

"I made you some oatmeal and a little ham that I cooked off. I know you have to be careful on game day, so I made things that would be easy on your stomach." He set the plate in front of Hunter and then sent his reminder texts and waited for the responses while he ate. Once he got them, he finished up and took care of the dishes before going up to change.

Monty put on his jersey over his T-shirt and brought a jacket in case it got chilly. Once he was ready, he looked in on Hunter, loaded the stuff in the car, and checked his mental list to ensure nothing was forgotten. The ring Hunter had given him was way too big, and rather than have it sized down, he wore it around his neck as a good-luck charm for Hunter. Finally he and Hunter were ready to leave.

At the stadium Monty dropped Hunter off and then parked in the player section. Fans were already tailgating and having a good time. Monty waited for Sue, and she escorted him through to the players' wives section.

"I see you have a jersey," Sue remarked.

"Hunter gave it to me, but I think it's closer to a football dress than a football jersey on me. I told Hunter I could cinch it and he nearly had a heart attack. So I left it."

"You're a trip," Sue said, and they found their seats and waited for the game to start. They had plenty of time, and Sue asked if he wanted a drink, but Monty was too nervous to eat or drink anything. Finally, with the roar of the crowd and an electricity in the air, the ball was kicked off and the game began.

"How much do you know about football?" Sue asked as Monty tried to follow what was happening.

"Hunter taught me the basics, but it's hard figuring out what they're doing."

"You don't understand football?" one of the other wives asked.

"This is Hunter's boyfriend," Sue said.

"Okay." The woman barely batted an eyelash at that. "But you don't understand football?"

You'd think Monty had just told her there was no Santa Claus and he'd just cooked the Easter Bunny for dinner.

"I have many other talents." Monty looked down his nose. "The only balls I'm really good with are attached, and I think Hunter really likes it that way." He turned back around and watched the field. The Red Hawks had the ball, and Monty watched them line up. "I really like this part."

"That's just getting into formation," Sue said.

"Come on. It's the 'looking at each other's butts' part. All I can say is that they better not be watching Hunter's or there will be some eye scratching going on."

175

"Stop that. I'm going to wet myself if you make me laugh any harder." She held her side as players raced around the field.

Someday Monty would figure this out. He saw the ball go high in the air, and all the Red Hawks fans were on their feet. "What happened?" Monty said, joining them.

"Hunter caught the pass. He's running, running, touchdown!" Sue jumped up and down, and Monty went right along with her. "Hunter scored!" She seemed beside herself, and Monty went wild, wriggling and swishing his hips in his own version of a happy dance.

"Don't you think that's a little swooshy?" one of the other wives asked.

"Back off," Sue said right away, and half the wives joined her, staring down the bleached blonde with enough cold to freeze Ecuador. She sat back down, and Monty turned his attention to the game, giving Sue a fist bump. He really liked her.

"Where are Petey and Davey?"

"With my mother." Sue didn't take her eyes off the field, and Monty settled in to watch and learn.

By halftime the Red Hawks were ahead by seven, and by the end of the third quarter, by seventeen. At that point Monty was starting to understand some of the game, and he could pick out Hunter wherever he was. So when Hunter caught another long pass and raced toward the goalpost thingies, he was on his feet. He cheered at the top of his lungs as Hunter scored his second touchdown of the day, with the crowd going wild. Half an hour later, the game was over.

"I think I get football now."

"You do?" Sue asked as they left their seats and headed toward the lower areas and the players' exit.

"Sure, I don't get the rules yet, but it was awesome as hell." He was so keyed up it was unreal, and he couldn't stand still.

They waited outside the locker-room area. The guys came out, talking and congratulating one another. Hunter approached, but Monty held back until they got outside and then jumped into his arms.

"You were so awesome. I think I can safely say that I love football." He whooped at the top of his lungs as Hunter beamed with pleasure and pride. "Can we go now?"

"You the man, Hunter," one of the players called as he passed. Monty didn't see which one because he was too intent on his amazing man.

"The playmaker!" someone else called from behind him.

"Yeah," Monty agreed. "You were the playmaker today."

"And you're my playmaker every day." Hunter pulled Monty down into a kiss.

ANDREW GREY grew up in western Michigan with a father who loved to tell stories and a mother who loved to read them. Since then he has lived all over the country and traveled throughout the world. He has a master's degree from the University of Wisconsin-Milwaukee and now works full-time on his writing. Andrew's hobbies include collecting antiques, gardening, and leaving his dirty dishes anywhere but in the sink (particularly when writing). He considers himself blessed with an accepting family, fantastic friends, and the world's most supportive and loving husband. Andrew currently lives in beautiful historic Carlisle, Pennsylvania.

E-mail: andrewgrey@comcast.net
Website: www.andrewgreybooks.com

CAN'T LIVE WITHOUT YOU

ANDREW GREY

Justin Hawthorne worked hard to realize his silver-screen dreams, making his way from small-town Pennsylvania to Hollywood and success. But it hasn't come without sacrifice. When Justin's father kicked him out for being gay, George Miller's family offered to take him in, but circumstances prevented it. Now Justin is back in town and has come face to face with George, the man he left without so much as a good-bye… and the man he's never stopped loving.

Justin's disappearance hit George hard, but he's made a life for himself as a home nurse and finds fulfillment in helping others. When he sees Justin again, George realizes the hole in his heart never mended, and he isn't the only one in need of healing. Justin needs time out of the public eye to find himself again, and George and his mother cannot turn him away. As they stay together in George's home, old feelings are rekindled. Is a second chance possible when everything George cares about is in Pennsylvania and Justin must return to his career in California? First they'll have to deal with the reason for Justin's abrupt departure all those years ago.

www.dreamspinnerpress.com

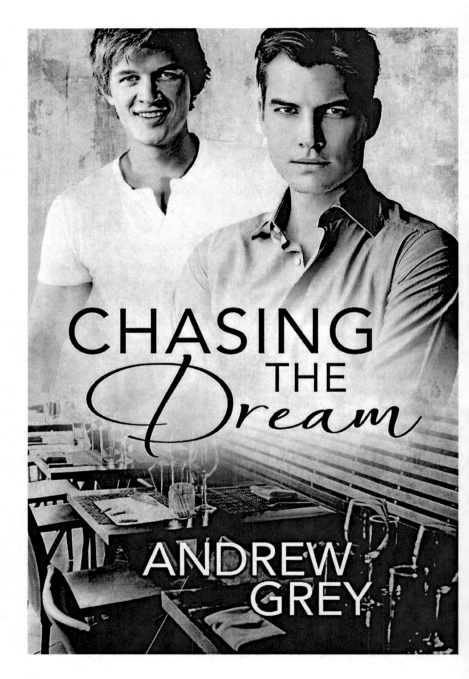

Born with a silver spoon in his mouth, Brian Paulson has lived a life of luxury and ease. If he's been left lonely because of his family's pursuit of wealth and their own happiness, he figures it's a small price to pay for what he sees as most important: money.

Cade McAllister has never had it easy. He works two jobs to support himself, his mother, and his special-needs brother. They don't have much, but to Cade, love and taking care of the people who are important to him mean more than material possessions. When Cade is mugged in the park, he can't afford to lose what little he has, and he's grateful for Brian's intervention.

Cade is given a chance to return the favor when Brian's grandfather passes away and Brian's assets are frozen. Cade offers Brian a place to stay and helps him find work, and the two men grow closer as they learn the good and the bad of the very different worlds they come from. Just as Brian is starting to see there's more to life than what money can buy, a clause in his grandfather's will could send their relationship up in smoke.

www.dreamspinnerpress.com

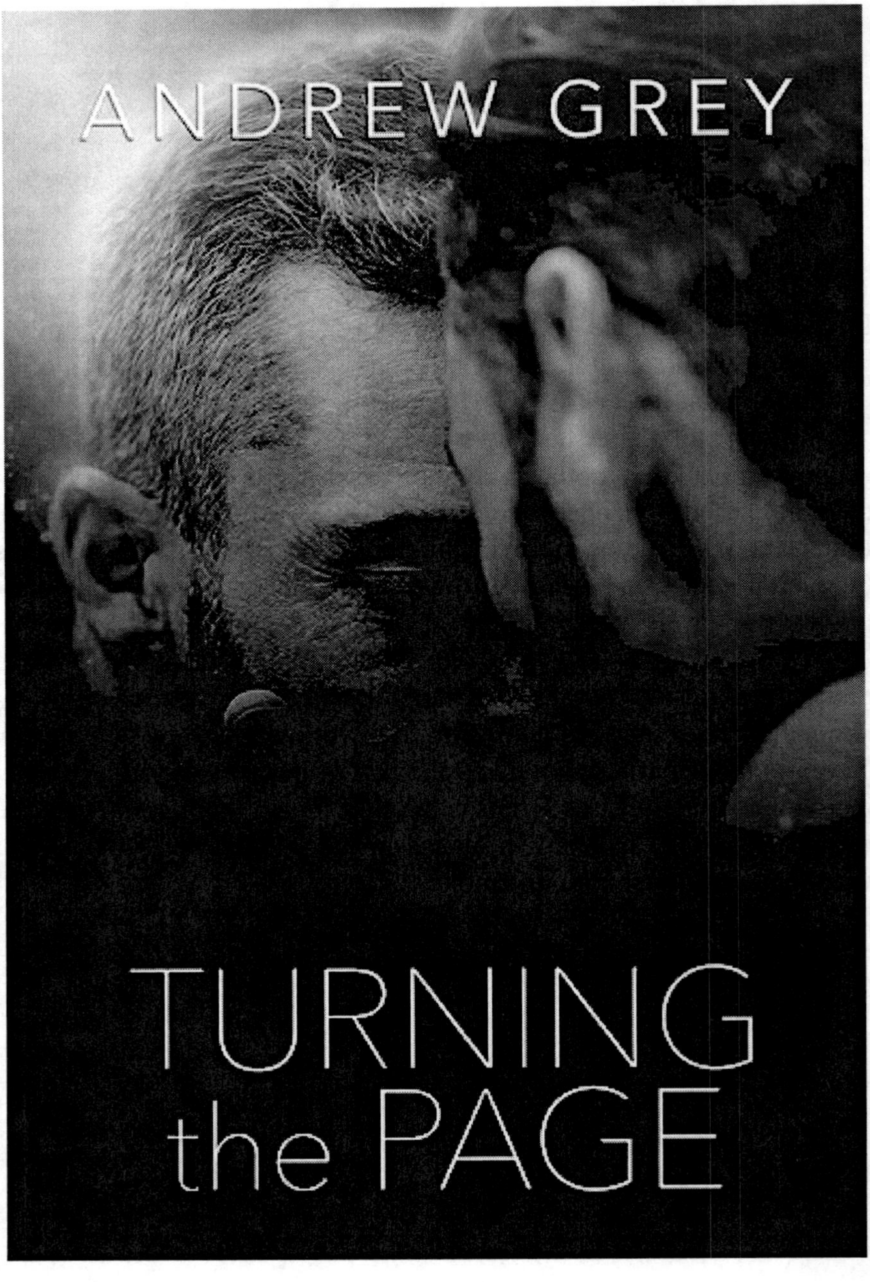
ANDREW GREY
TURNING
the PAGE

Malcolm Webber is still grieving the loss of his partner of twenty years to cancer. He's buried his mind and feelings in his legal work and isn't looking for another relationship. He isn't expecting to feel such a strong attraction when he meets Hans Erickson—especially since the man is quite a bit younger than him.

Hans is an adventure writer with an exciting lifestyle to match. When he needs a tax attorney to straighten out an error with the IRS, he ends up on the other side of the handsome Malcolm's desk. The heat between them is undeniable, but business has to come first. When it's concluded, Hans leaps on the chance to make his move.

Malcolm isn't sure he's ready for the next chapter in his life. Hans is so young and active that Malcolm worries he won't be able to hold his interest for long. Just when he's convinced himself to take the risk and turn the page, problems at the law office threaten to end their love story before it can really begin.

www.dreamspinnerpress.com

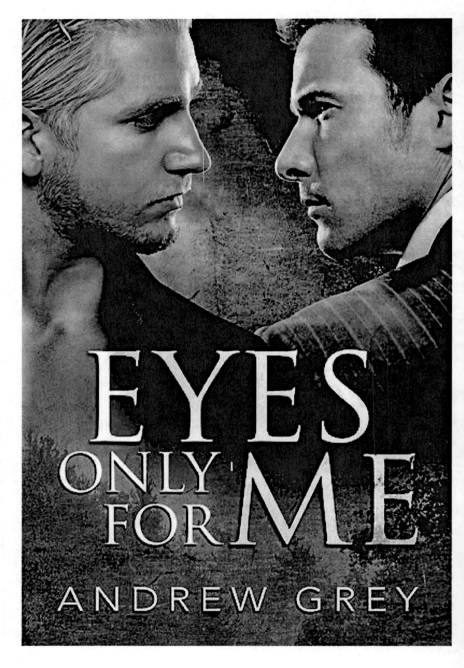

EYES
ONLY FOR ME

ANDREW GREY

Eyes of Love: Book One

For years, Clayton Potter's been friends and workout partners with Ronnie. Though Clay is attracted, he's never come on to Ronnie because, let's face it, Ronnie only dates women.

When Clay's father suffers a heart attack, Ronnie, having recently lost his dad, springs into action, driving Clay to the hospital over a hundred miles away. To stay close to Clay's father, the men share a hotel room near the hospital, but after an emotional day, one thing leads to another, and straight-as-an-arrow Ronnie make a proposal that knocks Clay's socks off! Just a little something to take the edge off.

Clay responds in a way he's never considered. After an amazing night together, Clay expects Ronnie to ignore what happened between them and go back to his old life. Ronnie surprises him and seems interested in additional exploration. Though they're friends, Clay suddenly finds it hard to accept the new Ronnie and suspects that Ronnie will return to his old ways. Maybe they both have a thing or two to learn.

www.dreamspinnerpress.com

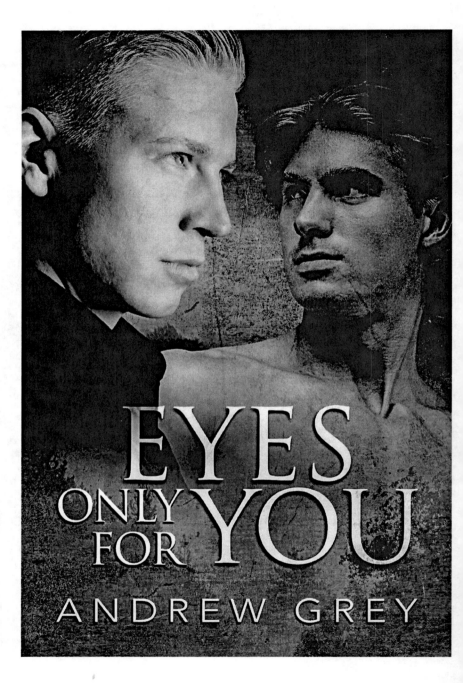

EYES
ONLY YOU
FOR

ANDREW GREY

Sequel to *Eyes Only for Me*
Eyes of Love: Book Two

Marcello Bagnini has a history of falling for the wrong men, and it seems he's done it again. Working out at the gym with his straight friend Jerry is becoming harder by the day—in more ways than one. Worse yet, Jerry isn't the only one who notices Marcello's wandering eyes. So instead of risking his friendship with Jerry and alienating the other guys at the gym, Marcello keeps his feelings to himself.

Real estate agent Jerry Foland has never explored his interest in other men, but there's something different about Marcello, and Jerry's starting to think he might like to see where his attraction could lead. However, Jerry's controlling father makes it clear that it's either stay on the straight and narrow or Jerry can say good-bye to his family.

As much as they try to stay away from each other, their lives overlap, both at the gym and when Jerry is contracted to sell the home of one of Marcello's friends. Friendship grows into more, but Jerry's father has his own agenda, and it doesn't include having a gay son.

www.dreamspinnerpress.com

FOR **MORE** OF THE **BEST GAY** ROMANCE

DREAMSPINNER
PRESS
dreamspinnerpress.com

CPSIA information can be obtained
at www.ICGtesting.com
Printed in the USA
FSOW02n1014201116
27625FS